CW01095545

DE**V**IL

KER DUKEY

Warning

This title deals with some sensitive subject matter and should be read with caution.

If you're a Ker Dukey reader/fan already, ignore this warning, as you're fucked up enough to not need it.

DEDICATION

We all have a little Devil in us, and even though your edges are frayed, the colors distorted in a mirage of uncertainty, to me you're a masterpiece.

~ Devil ~

Ker Dukey.

PROLOGUE

Evi

A shiver moves through me, causing every hair follicle to rise in awareness. My mind prowls into the dark corners where shadows hide the memories of my past.

The rasp of Garret's fingers flexing before tightening on the arm of the chair he sits in opposite me causes a stir in my stomach.

His tall, dominating presence when he's in doctor/patient mode quells any argument I'd usually throw his way when he wants me to open up about my past. I'm breathing heavily from thoughts of all that's transpired since I was last here with him, in his office.

He glances at me creeping his gaze over me, seeing right through to the marrow of my bones.

"Tell me what you remember from that night, Evi," he orders me. But I'm fighting the pull and shaking my head in response.

He uses my name with affection, his tone caressing the syllables, confusing me further.

The dynamics have shifted so much from patient/therapist that I don't know what's right and what's wrong anymore.

"You need to do this. It's time," he pushes, offering me a reassuring nod of his head.

His almond shaped orbs like a cat's prowl and probe, beckoning me to succumb.

But I don't want to. Instead, I want to beg him not to make me remember, but I know he's right.

It's time.

The sleepwalking has become too dangerous and the information from other people just doesn't add up.

The waves of memories haunting me don't make sense.

He won't let me avoid this any longer.

I don't want to avoid this. I need to know.

I need to know who I really am.

Fear seats itself in the forefront of my mind.

What if you don't like who you are?

"Remember. Tell me what happened," he demands, his voice hardening with authority.

My hands ball into fists as my heart thunders like a battle drum inside the prison of my chest.

Thud... Thud... Thud.

I focus on the balls swinging and clashing on the small Newton's Cradle that sits on the table beside me.

Closing my eyelids, I search the murky depths of my thoughts, wading in farther and farther.

Mirages flash before my senses. Disconnected, partial images, like swimming from dark water farther and farther toward the shoreline where the water clears and what lies beneath becomes unblemished, solid surface.

Color. Sound. Smell.

My insides seize and sorrow swells in my chest. Icy drops tap dance over my skin.

"Where are you, Evi?" Garret asks.

I'm there in the past, within the body of the old me, gasping for air in cracked, quivering breaths.

Small, broken.

I'm only a child, staring up at an endless black that spans before me.

"Tell me?" Garret's voice anchors me.

The sky expands before my pupils, a dusting of stars battling to shine through the thickening darkness of the night.

I'm so cold.

Too cold.

My body heavy, damp.

The concrete beneath me offers no comfort.

"I'm lying on the ground. I'm outside."

"Where outside?"

My observation flitters to the structure made up of discolored wood and glass. The terror, too horrifying to indulge the memory, battles to seat itself in my mind.

Strangers whispering, haunting my thoughts.

I know this place. I wish I didn't.

"It's my home. Our home. I'm in the yard of my old home," I choke.

Tangled strands of my wet hair stick to my head, hardening like cement. I lift my hand and the small digits show I'm young, a child.

My hand drops with a heavy thud.

The night has turned colder than any before it, blanketing me in an icy chill.

"I'm dying," I whisper.

I will be a frozen ghost if I don't get inside.

My body is weakening with every shallow breath I take in.

"You're okay. Breathe."

My body spasms, causing pain in my solidifying joints. My brain is willing me to move inside to the warm, but my limbs don't feel like my own and they refuse to obey my commands.

"I can hear something," I mutter.

It's faint but solid, so I cling to it.

"What do you hear, Evi?"

Hushed voices are sounding from an open window. My mouth peels open to call out to whoever it is, but it's only wasted breath, too quiet to be heard by anyone but me.

"I can't feel my legs. It's so cold."

There's a throbbing in my stomach but it doesn't compare to the expanding pit inside my chest.

It's too much pain. I'm screaming internally, wishing it would all end.

"You're okay. Keep going, Evi."

I don't want to. It hurts too much.

Hot tears pool and leak over my eyelashes, and I fight the memory so I don't have to face the crushing ache.

The pain opens in my ribcage; a black pit of sorrow, empty and consuming.

Reality floods in, the smell of Garret's aftershave and the warmth of his office.

I'm back in the room with Garret, not dying on the cold concrete floor. Lifting my hand, my perusal takes in the size of my palm. I didn't die. I'm a woman now.

"What are you feeling? Why did you come back, Evi?"

I shake my head, fighting him and myself mentally so I don't have to dissect this expanding ache.

"Don't make me feel it," I beg.

"Feel what? What is it you're feeling?"

A gasp escapes my lips as the pain from the memory washes over me like black rain, saturating me in its oily residue. I'll never get clean.

"What is it?"

"Grief." I grip my chest to make sure there's a heart still beating in there.

It's crippling, desperate sorrow, and it's drowning me from the inside out. I want to close myself off and fade into the heartache, never to resurface, but it's too late.

It's like I'm an intruder to the emotion. It's not mine to own. It's the little girl's who I abandoned when I forgot who she was.

Who *I* was.

"I'm dying!" I cry out.

Garret moves from his chair to kneel in front of me. Grasping my hand in his, he squeezes hard, producing enough pain to show me this is real and not the memory I'm living in.

"You're not dying. You didn't die, Evi. You were saved. Go back. Remember."

His words cocoon me in their safety. My lids flutter closed and I let the weight of my sorrow wrench me back there, the cold expanding over me like wet quicksand, swallowing me in the memory.

Footsteps slap against the wet surface around me and a boy's face appears, blocking the darkness of the sky.

"Someone is here."

"Who is it?"

My gaze is unfocused as I stare up at him. His features are distorted, like I'm looking through a misty window.

His voice as he breathes my name is familiar, though. I hold onto it, willing myself not to leave him.

"It's a boy."

"Here. Here!" His lips move, calling out into the night, desperation in his tone.

Other footfalls sound around me and a burst of sweet scent fills my nostrils.

"It's a woman's face now replacing the boy's. She's saying something."

"What is she saying?"

"She's alive! Get a paramedic out here now!" the woman shrieks.

Her warm hands caress the cold, tight skin of my cheek. Her calming voice holds affection I'm not used to.

"It's okay, sweetheart. You're going to be okay. Stay with me."

"Eleanor," I croak.

"Who's Eleanor, Evi?"

"Who's Eleanor, sweetie? Can you tell me where is she?"

Eleanor.

Other voices join hers, but my sight begins to cloud over and there's a humming in my ears.

"She's lost a lot of blood. We need to get her to the hospital now."

"I'm dying. Everywhere is numb."

"No, you're not. Stay with them, Evi."

"Did you find another girl inside? She's mumbling a name. Eleanor?" the woman mutters to someone out of sight.

Eleanor.

"No. Three males inside. No survivors."

My eyelids are too heavy; they're falling, pushing me under.

Eleanor.

Then there's nothing. The sky falls and swallows me into the obscurity.

Opening my eyes, dragging myself back from the memories, the name Eleanor is on my lips, but with it is a stabbing pain in my chest, so real I have to bring my hand there to rub the ache.

Shifting in his seat and clasping his hands together in his lap, Garret encourages me to go back.

"Stay with your memories, Evi. Take me to when you woke up," Garret tells me.

But I'm not sure I want to. The ghost pain is a warning, surely?

Silence hangs in the air like a thickening fog, filling the space around us.

Taking off his glasses and inspecting the lens, his lips part and my name whispers from his mouth, almost a plea. "Evi."

Ours gazes connect like magnets across the small space that separates us and he nods his head toward me to urge me on.

"Take us there, Evi. You're so close."

The waking up isn't a memory I can't recall. It's the only thing I actually remember vividly.

Closing my eyelids, the phantom smell of surgical soap assaults my senses. Waking up in hospital, or at all, was the most terrifying thing to happen to me.

Pain burns in my tummy; it's hot and sore. I want to cry out but my lips won't move; they're rough and stuck together like Velcro.

Forcing my eyelids to lift, they flutter when the light from overhead is too bright to let me focus.

My mind is numb, trying to grasp where I am. I come up empty.

My stomach drops and fear takes root. Panic flushes through me, as I remain trapped in this unaware state.

Where am I?

Who am I?

Pushing myself up from a lying position, I squint, taking in the room I'm in.

I'm in a bed with machines beeping around me and wires going into my hands.

Fighting with my thoughts for clues leaves me staring into a void. There's nothing.

Movement from a chair to my right catches my attention and a nurse frowns as she approaches me.

"Evi. You're awake."

"*Evi,*" I repeat, testing the name on my lips.

"You're in a hospital, but you're going to be just fine."

She's talking to me or at me, but I don't know who she is or who this Evi is she speaks of.

"Who's Evi?"

There's sadness in her gaze and a cautious tone to her speech.

"Can you tell me what you remember?"

My head swivels around the room scanning for another person she could be speaking to, but it's just me here.

Searching my thoughts for any information is like looking into a black abyss for a speck of dust.

There's a badge on the table next to me with a big number nine on, but apart from that there's nothing personal. No clues. Is that mine? Am I nine?

"Evi," she urges.

Who is Evi?

"Can you tell me what you remember?

Swallowing down the lump forming in my throat, I answer her with the truth.

"I don't remember anything."

I refocus my gaze on Garret and shrug with mourning. He pulls a tissue from the box in front of him and reaches forward to dab the tears I didn't know are falling over my lashes.

"I'm going to need you to really relax your mind now, Evi. Concentrate okay?"

"Okay."

"Go back to when you were on the ground and called out the name Eleanor. That's the same name you call out when you're sleepwalking. I want you to focus on the voices around you. Try to stay with them. Listen to them.

Close your eyes and go back."

Thud... Thud... Thud.

I do as he asks and close him out letting the dark night consume me.

"It's okay, sweetheart. You're going to be okay. Stay with me."

"Eleanor."

"Who's Eleanor, sweetie? Can you tell me where is she?"

Eleanor.

Voices swirl around me

"She's lost a lot of blood. We need to get her to the hospital now."

"Did you find another girl inside? She's mumbling a name. Eleanor?"

Eleanor.

"No. Three males inside. No survivors."

"I can't keep my eyelids open."

"Stay with them, Evi." Garret's voice penetrates my thoughts.

Eleanor.

Eleanor.

"She's her sister." The boy's familiar voice murmurs so softly it's like the whisper of snow hitting the ground.

Thud... Thud... Thud.

What? No. I don't have a sister.

Wait. Eleanor.

"No."

My body jolts, as if I've been struck by a thousand volts.

Memory after memory crashes into me, almost knocking me to the floor.

"Eleanor!" I cry out.

"Who is that, Evi?" Garret asks, his brow wrinkled.

"She was my sister, and the cause of everything."

CHAPTER ONE

LUCIFER

Evi

The calm of the water soothes me.

The cold compressing weight as I glide beneath its force is something otherworldly to me.

My lungs burn and tire, begging me for air, but I push myself further until the ache screams and the surface beckons me.

Gasping as I break the surface of the water, the corners of my mouth pulling upward.

The edge of life and death is so powerful; it burns adrenaline into the veins and causes the heart to roar like a beast within its cell.

I swim for the shoreline and already miss the water.

Cold air attacks my skin, akin to tiny spiders biting the exposed flesh. The liquid cascades down my body and leaves a puddle at my feet.

Every morning I swim, but the need to be in the water never wanes. It's as if I'm searching for something hidden in the fluid depths, but no matter how far I venture, I can never find it.

Taking a deep breath, I scan the water as it ripples in the wake of the humming breeze.

I love this time of the morning; the mist dancing over the lake as the trees sing to each other with the rustle of their leaves.

"You were out here again last night." A voice startles me.

My head whips to the tree line where Leroy Holst loiters.

Always watching, the sneaky little snake.

"This is private property, Leroy," I bark.

He begins swaggering toward me, his tall, willowy frame showing he's still a teen, yet to gain a more proportioned physique like his athletic father.

Picking up a stone and skipping it across the water, he comes too close for comfort, triggering my hands to clench.

"You don't own the lake, Evi!" He squints his beady stare at me in anger.

Bending down, he picks up another stone, bigger than the last, and lifts his arm to throw. Before he can, I reach up and grab his wrist firmly, adding enough pressure that his gaze snaps to mine, narrowing with every passing heave of his chest.

"Not the lake, but the land you're standing on right now? Mine."

He doesn't know boundaries, and whenever his parents visit their lake house, he always invades my land and privacy.

He has a chip on his shoulder when it comes to me, and I'm not entirely sure why I leave such a bad taste in his mouth.

I'm not really a people person, but that's why I stay on my own property and don't seek out his company.

Tugging his arm free and rubbing where my hand just was, he drops the stone at my feet. "Why are you always such a bitch?" he hisses, the spittle spraying over my face.

Disgusting little ass.

"Leroy Holst." A harsh voice bellows from the clearing that creates a pathway between the Holst's house and my own.

A man with the same eyes as the boy before me marches toward us.

Dr. Edward Holst—what a handsome man he is—even more so now there are age lines more prominent around his features since the death of their oldest son nearly a year ago.

Daniel Holst was believed to have drowned in the lake but his body was never recovered.

The complexities of the rapid drop in temperature the further you sink from the surface and the depths being so far down with hazards littering the lake floor make it almost impossible to find a body lost to the water. Not knowing exactly where he came off his boat didn't help the matter, and the fact he wasn't reported missing until the next day.

They may never have closure.

I know how that feels.

A shiver races through my blood, producing a sprinkle of tiny hairs to rise over my body.

The nippy chill in the air wraps itself around me like a frozen blanket.

"I'm sorry, Evi. Is he being a pest again?" he asks, his footfalls coming to rest beside his son's.

His gaze bores a hole in the side of Leroy's cheek.

I offer a small smile, folding my arms and suddenly feeling at a disadvantage being the only one standing in almost nothing and sopping wet to boot.

"Nothing I can't handle, Edward. You're here early this year?"

It's a statement but I pose it as a question.

His stare drags to mine and he smiles tightly, nodding his head.

"Yes, Jacqueline was anxious to get here. She feels closer to Daniel here." Sadness expands his pupils as they drift to stare out at the lake.

Leroy makes a scoffing sound and glowering in my direction.

"It's morbid and I don't see why I have to be here. I'm

seventeen, for God's sake." He kicks at the shingle beneath his foot.

Turning to his son, Edward grasps his chin between his forefinger and thumb, holding him hostage, his strength and height dominating.

My insides flip and buzz with energy, and shaming arousal pools in my stomach at his performance.

"And yet you act like a seven-year-old. You will be wherever your mother wants you to be. Have some respect."

Pushing his father's hand away, Leroy storms off into the trees.

"Sorry you had to witness that. He struggles with his brother's death and doesn't know how to deal with it."

He should see a therapist.

I force myself to look away from the good doctor and scan over the lake surface. The thought of Daniel's body being out there somewhere doesn't deter me from swimming in the water.

Daniel was a weak swimmer and shouldn't have been allowed on the lake by himself, even at nineteen.

He was clumsy and liked to drink while fishing. Idiot.

They dragged the lake but the water is too deep; brush litters the endless depths and the temperature drops so much that bodies, instead of becoming bloated and rising, become frozen and sink. They can take years to show up, if ever.

"Death changes people," I state.

"I need to go dry off before I freeze." I give him a slight smile, gesturing down my body to show I'm in just my swimsuit in case he hadn't noticed.

I'm trying to be as polite as possible, but with the intent of just getting away. I don't deal well with death and I'm not really good with idle chitchat. That's why coming here off-season is perfect for me.

That was until the Holst's began arriving weeks in advance.

He observes me scanning over my attire, which is a plain black one-piece, but it's cold and my nipples are tenting the fabric.

He hovers at them for a second more than he should when giving me the once over.

Naughty thoughts, Dr. Edward?

Shaking his head, he quickly looks away, embarrassed, and says, "Of course. See you later, Evi," over his shoulder as he returns to his house.

The arousal from earlier reignites inside me, causing an ache I need to relieve.

Racing up to the house, I strip from my wet suit, peeling it down my sticky, moist body.

The air is warm in here and skips over my skin like warm kisses.

Dropping onto the sofa I lift my feet, placing them on the coffee table spreading them and letting my hands stroke down to my exposed pussy, parting the lips and teasing my clit.

Dr. Edward's gaze fixated at my nipples earlier plays over and over, bringing me to climax.

With the release comes the shame, and I want to go wash off the sins in the lake; purify myself. Instead, I get to my feet and grab my swimsuit from the pile I left it in. There's a small puddle seeping into the wood floor, distorting the color, and I become fixated.

Blood. So much blood, pooling like spilt milk.

The phone shrills and I startle, pulling my care from the water mess.

I check the caller ID and pick up and place it straight back down.

I've been getting ghost calls from an unknown number for a couple of weeks now. No one ever speaks but I hear the breathing and my own voice saying "Hello" crackle down the line.

Hanging my swimsuit over an airer to dry, I make my way to the shower and blast it as hot as it will go.

The steam fills the room and hides the glow of my self-inflicted pleasure as I wash away the disgrace under the raining heat.

CHAPTER TWO

SATAN

I sit and then stand, anxious more than curious of the box that's been sitting there on the table since It arrived here four days ago, its ratty cardboard fraying and peeling at the edges.

It's my birthday, and my mother said to open the box on my twenty- first birthday. Maybe I should wait for Garret to get here and have him open it.

My thoughts move to Garret and the anniversary of our relationship fast approaching. He wants more from me but doesn't understand why I wouldn't be ready for such things as marriage and children, despite him being a therapist. *My* therapist.

He knows how I feel about not knowing who I really am, who I come from. It's a discombobulating emotion.

I don't feel like a complete person. I'm particles of a whole but the whole is fragmented and floating like dust particles caught in the stream of light, visible only when it shines through a crack in a window.

My adoptive parents have been wonderful, and not remembering anything about my family before them made it easier to bond with them, but there has always been a disconnect with any attachments I make.

A murky cloud haunts me in the back of my subconscious, warning me that those you let close can hurt you worse than any other.

My cell chimes, alerting me to a text from Garret. Already knowing it's going to be him delaying his visit due to work, I don't even read it.

He's a doctor, so patients always come first.

"Evi, you know the boundaries I have to form for this to work out."

Boundaries are always a thin line and I've never met one person who hasn't crossed them.

My fingers dance over the rough edges of the worn box urging me to open it and learn from the contents, but instead I abandon the thing and go make some food.

What's inside?

Flicking the iPod on to my lake house playlist, soft melodies fill the silent space and croon around me, comforting me like a warm hug.

If I concentrate on the lyrics and instruments, my mind won't wander into the dangerous places that will hold me hostage in their darkness.

The empty time in the afternoon is always hardest for me to fill; boredom sets in motion bad behavior and cravings I shouldn't have.

But nighttime—nighttime is where I become prisoner to past wounds howling in the moonlight to be heard.

I don't give in to the demons clawing at the surface of my reality. Instead, I live the lie. I live this person I created after waking up in the hospital all those years ago without knowing who I was before.

I wish I could start over. Be someone else. Choose who I was created from, but I'm no God and this is no fairy tale.

My stomach growls and hunger pains follow, cramping my muscles. Cooking was something I enjoyed and was good at.

I go to the fully stocked cupboards and pull out the ingredients for cheesy pasta bowl, filling a pan with hot water and lighting the stove.

I'm just pouring in the dried shells when a familiar inkling heightens my senses.

Thud...

The awareness of being watched stiffens my posture as I move the pan from the hob and walk toward the window.

If that little snake is watching me again…

I peer outside but the sun has begun to set and my own reflection surrounded by darkness is all I see staring back at me.

Don't let him in

My appetite diminishes and I find myself tossing the food I just began to prepare into the trash.

Pushing through the front door, I watch the sun set over the lake and try to ebb the intense feeling of being observed by unwanted appreciation.

This all feels so familiar, like it's a rehearsal I'm repeating.

Don't let him in

A snapping twig signals from the brush and gains my attention.

"Daniel?" I call out.

"Daniel?" Leroy scoffs bitterly, coming into view. "Is that a joke?"

My heart speeds up and then settles when I see who it is.

"Leroy. I meant Leroy. I'm sorry." I shake my head, guilt seeping out of me even though he's trespassing on my property again.

"It's fine." He shrugs. "Mom says we look the same. Could have been twins."

I don't agree.

Daniel was taller and had a more masculine form. Lifting weights for lacrosse had given him a strong, de-fined physique, whereas Leroy is slim and breakable.

"What are you doing out here?" I ask, my tone accusing.

"Getting some wood. We're going to make a pit and cook barbecue."

He just stands there, no wood collected because he's been too busy looking through my windows.

"Why are you getting wood here and not on your own property line?" I growl out through clenched teeth.

Folding his arms over his chest, he spits on the ground and sneers. "Because my dad told me to invite you over."

My stomach twists with pain from not eating. It's their son's fault I'm starving right now and not eating.

I guess it won't be too painful to sit with them for an hour and get fed.

"I could eat." I watch with enjoyment as his eyebrows nearly meet his hairline.

"I told him you wouldn't come."

"Well, I'm hungry."

Going back inside to grab a sweater slung on the couch, I return to find Leroy has left.

Jerk.

The smell of flame-grilled meat thickens in the air the closer I get to the Holst's household.

Golden licks of light shine through clearings in the trees.

Edward sees me before anyone else and he pokes at some food on the barbecue with a giant fork.

"Evi. Leroy said you weren't coming." He looks over his shoulder at his son, who's slouched in a deckchair, holding a stick over the fire pit they've made.

"She must have changed her mind," Leroy grates out.

I move closer and stand awkwardly, already regretting my choice.

"Well, I'm glad she did. I could do with some adult conversation." Edward winks at me and gestures with his free hand to one of the three deckchairs in a circle around the fire.

Leroy jumps up from his seat, making a show of tossing down his stick. That's when I realize it has a mallow stuffed on the end and it's now melting into the mud like wax from a candle.

"You do know she's closer to my age than yours, right?" He snorts at his father.

Plating up the food he's been cooking, Edward places it on a table next to me and ignores him.

"Evi, plates are over there. Help yourself."

The meat sizzles next to me and the smell is intoxicating, initiating a burst of saliva to form over my tongue.

The sound of the front door swinging open and crashing closed signals Leroy's departure.

I squirm in my seat, knowing I invaded their space, and I'm now left alone with the doctor.

Grabbing a plate and fork from the small pile stacked next to the barbecue, I fill my plate with steak and sausage and then take the seat offered to me.

Edward follows suit and beams over at me from the few feet that separate us.

"It's nice to see a girl eat real food. Jacqueline always insists on a salad."

I swallow down the mouthful I'd just shoved in and ask, "Will she not be joining us?"

Frown lines mar his forehead and he studies his food without eating it.

"I doubt it. No mother should have to outlive their child, and it makes it all the more difficult not having his remains to bury. The thought of him being out there all alone… it breaks her daily."

Grief slams into me, nearly buckling me over. I drop the plate of food and stand abruptly. "I need to go."

Edward gets to his feet, placing his plate on the seat behind him and holding his hands out toward me as you would an injured animal, scared and trying to flee.

"I'm sorry. It's morbid, I know." He voice is heavy with sadness.

"I just… I'm sorry." I dart off toward the trees and flinch when a twig scrapes across my leg, but I don't stop.

My feet pick up pace until I'm running back to my house and slamming the door closed.

My breathing is labored, my lungs squeezing, restricting my airflow.

The room spins and I wobble on my feet until I collapse on the couch, sucking in oxygen.

My eyelids droop closed and faint, like voices from a choir muffled by closed church doors, I hear crying.

It beckons me.

CHAPTER THREE

PRINCE OF DARKNESS

Cold. So intense that I shiver and rub at my arms to warm up, but the friction causes the skin to tear and I'm bleeding.

Crying from a child, loud and piercing, stabs at me until sorrow seeps from my pores like blood from an open vein.

I'm bleeding out. I'm dying. Kill me.

A shrill noise drowns out the sobs of the child and it's calling me like a flare in the ocean. I follow until it's loud and prominent in my mind, blocking out everything else. Reality washes over me.

I'm dreaming.

My eyelids try to lift but they feel weighted down with concrete as I try to pry them open. I need to wake up.

Pushing myself to a sitting position, I force myself to rouse fully.

The light from overhead burns my retinas as they finally open and gloss over with a sheen of tears. I swipe away the water droplets forming and breathe in gulps of air.

Taking in my surroundings, the quirky furniture and muted colors signal that I'm at the cabin, and flashes of me coming home and having a mild panic attack remind me that I must have fallen asleep.

Noise pricks my ears, the shrilling sound from my dream. Scanning the room, I follow the sound until I'm at the computer. It's a Skype call.

Getting to my feet, the groggy pull of tiredness causes me to stumble a little, but I make it to the other side of the room and click the link when I see that it's Garret calling.

A box opens and his flawless porcelain skin stretched over perfect symmetry features greets me.

Blue orbs decorated with a flutter of dark lashes blink a couple of times as he studies the woman staring back at him.

My image sits like a mirror reflecting back at me in the corner.

My hair is a tangle of dark curls on top of my head in the hairband I used to create a messy bun after my shower earlier.

The dark of my eyes are a direct contrast to the light of his.

My lips are full and pouting, his in a straight line,

giving away no emotion.

"You look tired. Are the sleeping pills not helping?" Garret asks, concern lacing his tone.

My gaze falls to the clock, the time in the right hand corner of my screen.

He's wearing a work suit, despite it being almost ten at night.

The grey pinstripes pull over the thick muscle beneath. I can't see all of him, but I don't have to to know what's there.

"They make me sleep walk," I admit with a yawn.

"Have you had any incidents?" He gets closer to the screen, to penetrate me with his concerned stare. When he's this close, I can see the dark circles forming under his bottom lashes.

He works too late and doesn't give himself enough time to relax. I could help him with that if he were here.

"No. I'm fine. Everything is fine." I shrug, wiping a hand over my brow, still feeling the slight burn from the light intrusion moments before.

My feet flex as I straighten my legs and stretch. Everything is tight and bound like an overworked spring.

"Have you opened the box?"

His voice cocoons around me and strokes over places already sore from my own touch.

"Evi."

He says my name sharply to grasp my attention. He always knows when my mind is wandering to bad places.

"Can you focus and answer my question?"

"What did you ask?"

The sigh from his lips whispers over my own and I have to bite my lip to stop myself from spiraling.

"Did you open the box?"

I scan the room, locating the box he speaks of.

"No. I was hoping you would come open it for me." I half smile.

He smiles tightly in return and shakes his head. "It wouldn't make seeing what's inside any easier."

How would he know?

"Maybe it would."

"You're welcome to bring it here." He raises a brow and then rubs at the small growth of hair on his chin. He's been working too much; it's outgrown the usual length he keeps it.

A yawn pushes past my lips. "You know I hate the city."

His eyes sparkle mischievously. "Maybe you would learn to love it."

Can you learn to love things?

"Maybe you would learn to love the wilderness if you spent more time in it. We could swim in the lake and barbecue our dinner. Hike, and then finish our nights making love in front of the fire."

He exhales and uses his middle fingers to massage his temple while closing his eyelids for a moment.

"My profession, Evi. It's important…" I hold up my hand to cut off his tirade about how important his work is. It's the same conversation on a different day.

"It's my birthday for only two more hours and you haven't even wished me a happy one." I opt for giving him the doe look I know affects him because his own eyes always soften in response.

Leaning back in his chair, he folds his arms. His shirt-sleeves are rolled up to his forearms and those veins men have in their arms bulge with the strain.

I want to climb through the screen and mount him, make him bend to my will, mess up that perfectly styled hair, and cause those crystal orbs to darken with lust.

"Evi, are you even listening to me?"

"No. I wasn't," I answer truthfully, wishing he would shut up and rip open that shirt, sending all those buttons in different directions and advertising the granite muscles beneath.

He laughs; it's broad and sincere. "I do admire your honest tongue."

He would admire my tongue in a more pleasing manner if he just came here. I want to suck him like he's an ice pop and I'm dehydrating on a hot summer's night.

"I said you should get some rest. We can pick this up tomorrow."

Don't go. Stay and play with me.

"You still haven't wished me a happy birthday." I pout, needy and sticky all over with a sheen of sweat caused by lust.

I watch as the screen appears to dull and he shifts in his seat.

"Garret?"

He doesn't answer.

My gaze lingers on the screen, searching, and then movement causes me to lose my breath.

I watch, mesmerized, as he begins to lower the monitor

to his lap.

A thick outline signals his hard cock and my nipples peak and ache for his touch.

My chest seizes and my pussy throbs with need.

He unzips his slacks, slow and torturous, and I can hear my own heart thundering inside my chest.

The pulse between my thighs pumps in unison.

His cock springs free, thick and long, the end a shiny, bulging mushroom head, begging for my lips to taste the clear liquid beading of pre-cum. Wide, paw-like hands wrap neatly around the girth. Leisurely strokes trail the length, gliding over the tip, spreading the juices, and my fingers slip into my panties to ease the ache pounding there.

Rubbing against my needy clit, tingles shoot through my legs, all the way down to my toes.

I'm wet and my hands slip easily through my folds, teasing the swelling, needy hole.

He's fisting his cock, stroking harder and harder, forcing my fingers to do the same.

A sound of an incoming text message steals my attention for a second, my head swiveling to the offending cell phone on the coffee table.

When I look back to the screen, there's just a fuzzing of black and white static on the screen. Damn it. We must have lost signal.

Walking over to my cell, I snatch it up, feeling like I could explode. I'm tense all over and the old feeling of shame begins warming my cheeks.

I read the message once and then again.

Happy Birthday, Evi. Get some sleep.

How the hell did he text that while on chat. Dropping the cell, a frustrated sigh leaves my lips. The box from my mom glares at me for attention and I decide it's time to see inside.

CHAPTER FOUR

FIEND

Boiling a pot of water I pour the hot liquid into the mug and dunk the teabag in and out. Garret says herbal tea will help me sleep better but I think it just keeps me awake.

Maybe that's what he wants so I won't sleepwalk again.

I've often woken up in a state of panic, not knowing where I am when the dreams take hold so vividly that my body follows my mind.

Wrapping my hands around the mug, I sip the hot liquid and then put it down, grabbing up the box and placing it on the couch before sitting beside it and staring at it.

Just open it, Evi.

I pry the lid from its stuck down position. It comes away with a jolt.

A musky scent like an old bookshop full of second hand Mills and Boon books fills my nostrils and causes me to sneeze.

I hate the smell of old cardboard.

There's a tremble in my hand as I grip the lid tightly and peer inside.

Thud...

Documents sit on top of a pile of paperwork. Bold letters forming words stare back at me from the top page.

Adoption of Evi Devil.

Evi Devil? *Devil?*

So my birth name is Evi and my new parents kept it. I was given my adoptive parents last name—Reed—but the name Devil glares up at me, turning my stomach to a bubbling acid pit and ingraining itself onto my soul.

Devil.

Evi Devil.

Who the hell were my parents?

Is that a real name or one they changed to Devil?

My date of birth is listed and matches the date I've always celebrated.

There's an article that has my heart slowing as I pull it free.

Mother massacres her own family
Only survivor is nine-year-old daughter who
recovers in hospital from a stab wound to the
abdomen.

Dropping the newspaper clipping, my head pounds, my skull shrinking and suffocating my brain.

Flashes like glimpses of a speeding train wash through my mind but there's nothing solid, just scraps that don't make sense. My thoughts are the enemy, like a jumbled mess of jigsaw pieces that don't go together. Even if I ordered them to make a picture, the picture would never be complete. Forced memories created from scraps to form an image.

Picking the clipping back up, I continue to read.

The controversial case of Melanie Devil, a mother accused of the brutal massacre of her own family and attempted murder of her daughter ended in court today with a verdict of a guilty plea.

<u>*Thud...*</u>

Melanie was sentenced to four life sentences.

<u>*Thud...*</u>

Being led out of the courthouse by officers to begin her sentence in the Central maximum-security prison. Reports confirm Miss Devil was given a full psychological evaluation clearing her of any mental illness.

<u>*Thud...*</u>

In her testimony that was read out in court Miss Devil offered no apologises. Claiming her family were impure.

"What prompts a person to take the life of

**innocent children is something we may never
understand,"** County police said in a statement

I crunch the paper in my fist, unable to read the rest
of the words. I get to my feet, racing toward the front door
and bursting through it, gasping for oxygen to fill my tightening chest.

The night air greets me, lapping over my skin; the
moon big and full casts a blue glow over the calm water.

My heart is almost visible as it pounds violently in my
ribcage.

I knew my family had died; my adoptive parents told
me as much, but I never knew how or by whose hand.

Not having memories from that time left me blank for
information.

No name to follow up on, no old addresses to seek out.
No family I could remember.

I was a new person and that was a past life.

My nerves settle, the vibrations in my skin from the
blood pumping through them hums to a slow beat.

The water calls to me. *Wash away the pain.*

Something within the water catches my eye so I pull all
my focus to the spot; it's clothing or… someone.

Daniel...

Racing down the steps and over the rocky stone path
to the water's edge, I focus on the water scanning it for
what I saw moments before, but there's nothing.

The surface is clear and undisturbed. Hairs rise on the
back of my neck as goose bumps scatter over my flesh.

A rustling and then footfalls sound from behind me.

Spinning to see who is approaching at this time of night, I take a protective stance.

Sighing, I hold a hand to my chest. "You scared me."

"I'm sorry. That wasn't my intent. I saw you running down to the water and it's so late I was worried you may have…" He drifts off, searching the water.

Why was he watching my house?

"How did you see me, Edward?" I ask, looking through the brush at the darkened house he owns.

"I couldn't sleep. I was on the porch just watching the stillness."

I bow my head. I know all about not being able to sleep, only I never know I've fallen asleep until I wake in strange places I have no memory of going to.

"Evi." He says my name like a plea and it stirs my stomach.

"What?" I breathe.

"You're bleeding." He looks down at my feet. There's a crimson puddle forming under the sole of my foot.

"I must have cut it on the rocks."

He bends down and lifts my foot, inspecting the underneath.

"I can't really see in this light. Let's get you inside."

Before I can object, he's lifting me bridal style into his arms and carrying me back inside.

His hot palms burn a fire over my thigh and thoughts of him throwing me down and ravishing me echo through my mind.

It's not what I want to happen, it's almost like it's what I expect to happen.

Placing me down on my couch, he goes to my kitchen and begins looking in the cupboards.

"First aid is in the bathroom," I offer, feeling crowded despite the space between us.

His footsteps carry through the house and then he's back, placing the first aid box on the table and pulling out cleaning swabs and bandages. The veins bulge in his forearms with his movements and Garret comes to mind. What would he think of Dr. Edward being here when *he* should be here instead?

Sitting opposite me, he takes my ankle in his palm and brings my leg up to rest on his knee.

His regard lifts briefly to my dress that has gathered at the top of my thighs, exposing a glimpse of my cotton panties.

Clearing his throat, he tells me, "It doesn't look too bad, but a couple of stitches are required. I should go get my medical bag."

Looking down to see the wound for myself, I frown. I can't even feel it, but he's right; there's a nasty gash seeping with blood that's created a stain on his pants.

Drip. Drip. Drip.

"Evi, did you hear me?"

Pulling my gaze from the blood, I nod my head in response.

His lips lift and he pats my knee softly like a doctor to a patient, or a father to his child.

"I'll be right back and have you fixed up in no time."

The room expands as he leaves and I feel tiny within its confines.

A crimson display on the sole of my foot draws me in, mesmerizing me.

By the time Edward gets back, he's flustered, his cheeks red, and a littering of sweat beads along his hairline.

For a man who works out often and is still in his prime, he appears to be sweating and out of breath.

I'm not completely void of the effect I have on men.

It made me a target for bullying in school by popular girls who didn't like the way their boyfriend's gapes would follow my movements.

Garret had brought it up a few times in our sessions about the sensuality I display without being conscious of it, but it isn't my fault.

I don't project that with intent.

I don't want the advances I'm often faced with.

Men are just visual creatures and their desires rule over anything else. It's useful from time to time, and the heady sensation of bringing a grown man like Edward down to his basic need is empowering.

If I choose it, I could make him give in, break his vows, destroy his own will.

Men like Edward always invoke a heady sensation to take over me. My body craves their attention without permission; my mind knows it's wrong but my body thinks for her slutty self.

Garret was reluctant to link it back to my childhood. Saying it stems back to my childhood and the abuse I suffered is unethical.

"There's a reason you associate men with authority as sexual creatures, and they affect you on this level due to

issues you no doubt had with your father."

The small scar between my thighs hums with his words.

"Because he abused me?"

"I can't comment that this stems from abuse, Evi."

He didn't need to confirm his thoughts with the correct words; his diagnosis was clear.

But if I don't remember being abused, how can it affect me in such ways?

He never seemed to have an answer to that question.

"I can't make premature conclusions about your memories. I can't interpret your past because that can influence forced memories."

Edward's tight smile as he repositions himself in front of me brings my focus back to him. The flush in his cheeks as he lifts my ankle once more is almost comical.

This man is a doctor; he must have been in situations where he has seen more than a flash of a girl's panties while fixing her up before. But it's amusing and hot to see the reaction from him; the reaction little me provokes in him.

I watch, transfixed as his gaze that keeps flitting to the exposure between my thighs, my dress having fallen around my waist, my panties on display for his greedy observation. Like father, like son. Peeping toms.

When he swipes his tongue out to wet his bottom lip, I find myself reacting to him.

My nipples harden and I think about what he would do if I slid my hands into my panties and stroked myself right in front of him.

Can he smell my arousal; see the wet essence glistening

along the line of my panties?

Knowing I'm creating a damp patch where he can see causes my heart to thunder and my breath to become heavy.

The pulse throbs through my body, ending in my clit that ticks like a time bomb waiting to explode.

"I'm going to numb the area," he tells me, his tone hoarse with his own thick arousal.

The atmosphere in the room has shifted, the air heavy and hot. My head is like a carousel, spinning with possibilities and conflicting need to come and to clean myself of these bad thoughts.

Lust dilutes his pupils, his tongue constantly moistening his lips. He's in need, lonely, desperate for contact.

It must be hard living with a grieving wife. Even before their son's death, she wasn't the warmest of women.

Thoughts of him fucking his receptionist, maybe a patient here and there, sends my hormones spiraling inside me.

Naughty doctor.

"You don't need to use anything. A little bit of pain lets us know we're alive," I breathe with a sultry purse of my lips.

He's not sure if I'm being flirty or just brave and it makes me giddy. His scrutiny pins me to the seat, studying me.

"I don't want to hurt you."

A simper curls the side of my lip.

Why? Hurt me, Edward.

"I'm a big girl, Edward. Just push it in already."

I relish the small gasp he takes at my words, referring to the needle he has gotten ready to use to stich up the small gash.

When his stare once again drops to my panties, I drop my knees a little more, giving him a better look.

I wonder if he feels like a pervert; I'm only a couple of years older than his sons. The bulge in his trousers excites me further. I did that to him and he got so caught up in just a glimpse that he couldn't control his body.

Look what I made you do. Who has the power?

"Doctor?" I say, in a sultry slur, wiggling my toes to bring his attention back to my bleeding foot and to let him know I've caught him putting his attention elsewhere.

He startles and the crimson stain on his cheeks spreads into his hairline.

"Okay. You ready?"

"I've been ready for a while now. I'm dripping, Edward."

"What?" He exhales, his pupils dilating and glazing over and his once steady hand trembling as he drops his gawk back to the junction between my thighs. I hold back my amusement, tilt my head to the side, and point my finger to the blood dripping between his legs.

"Oh, hell."

Grabbing some cotton balls, he cleans up the mess.

I've grown bored of this game now and want my foot sewed up so he can give it back to me.

As handsome as he is, I'm not desperate enough or horny enough to play games and follow this through with a man who's old enough to be my father, and whose grieving wife is a short walk away.

I'm a contradiction some days. I can't keep up with my revolving thoughts.

My attention drifts to the box I opened earlier and the name Devil springs into my mind in big neon lights.

"Have you ever heard of anyone with the last name Devil?" I query, knowing he is a worldly man.

His brow furrows at my question. "It's a rare name. French decent, I believe."

"So you have heard of it before?"

I thought it might have been a made up name.

He's concentrating on my foot and pulling what looks like string through the skin and tying it.

"I've heard it once, in the papers. Going back at least a decade now."

My hands grip the couch cushions at his confession.

Coincidence?

"How could you remember something like that?" I laugh in jest, but the edge in my voice gives away the nerves.

He seems too busy with his mending to notice. He hums and taps his finger a couple of times against the skin on one of my toes while in thought.

"It was a pretty memorable story." His stare briefly flits to mine before going back to my foot.

"A woman lost her mind and killed her husband and children. Apparently they were legally called Devil and they took the name literally. A house of horrors, according to the newspaper." He shudders.

"You can't always believe what you read in the papers

though, right?" I laugh, feeling anything but humor inside my bones.

Rubbing the corners of the plaster bandage he has placed over my wound, he shrugs. "The woman confessed. Open and shut case, I believe."

"I can't believe you remember something like that." I observe, taking my foot from his lap. His head tilts to the side, studying me. "It being so long ago," I clarify.

"I only remember because it was in the next town and our boys were young. It's hard to understand a parent being capable of harming their children."

Nodding my head, I pull my dress down over my thighs.

In the next town over? So close.

"Thank you for fixing me up."

Getting to his feet, he begins putting his medical things back in his bag.

The atmosphere has become awkward, neither of us knowing what to say now. It almost feels like we've done something wrong when, in reality, we didn't bite the forbidden apple.

"I should get back before anyone wakes up and wonders where I am."

Would they care? I think, but don't speak the words.

I follow him to the front door and he turns last minute and grasps my waist to his body, smothering me.

He is so much taller than me; it's only so noticeable now that he's almost on top of me like I'm wearing him as a coat.

My breath hitches when I realize his lips are descending

over my open mouth in a hungry, needy kiss. I didn't think he would have the balls to act on his desire, but his spontaneous approach catches me off guard and my body doesn't know whether to resist or roll with it.

I let him kiss me, feel his body, needy and hard against my stomach. The scruff on his chin scrapes and burns my soft skin but I allow him his fill, knowing his reality will come flooding in, and within a few seconds, he pulls away, wide-eyed and jittery.

"I'm sorry. I… that… I shouldn't have."

Wiping my thumb over my wet bottom lip, I just stare at him, letting all the chaos collide and spin around in his head.

"I should go."

Stepping out onto the porch, I watch him practically run through the brush back to his own house.

Dr. Edward Holst lost control. Perversion must run in the family.

I think about the possibility of Leroy watching through the window, catching his father battling his need and losing.

What would Garret think about that?

My attention drifts to the lake and search for whatever it was I saw out here earlier that caused me to run to the water and cut myself. It's calm and black, like oil instead of water.

A yawn passes my lips and it reminds me of how late it is.

My thoughts drift to Edward and his family.

Will he be weird around me? Will he have a guilty

conscious and tell his wife? Or will he harbor desire and act on it again? I'm unsure one way or the other, or how I would react to any or all of those scenarios.

Although I'm young, sex isn't new to me. From an early age, I'd had desire.

It was usually when I'd find boys watching me, looking at my small tits still in a training bra. Or when my English teacher would walk past my desk and purposely knock my pencil to the floor so I'd have to bend over to retrieve it, giving him an eyeful of my backside when my skirt would ride up.

It was a tingling, a satisfaction to flaunt myself, make them want me. Almost like validation, only once I'd given in to acting out those fantasies, I felt wrong and dirty, and gravitated toward the water to cleanse and swim.

My adoptive parents, Harold and Kate, knew there was something about me lurking under the pretty they worked so hard to achieve.

Harold had once walked in on me in the tub and my instinct told me to remain still, not to cover up my body.

He was mortified and quickly left and wouldn't speak or look at me over the dinner table for three days.

Garret told me my sexual urges stem from trauma from my life before I was adopted, but how can something affect my character now if the person I was then doesn't exist anymore?

Locking the front door, I go to my room, willing my body to tire enough for sleep.

Stripping naked, I stand in front of the full-length mirror in my bedroom and scan the form reflecting back at me.

My skin tone is a rich olive color. I always assumed I was Italian with my dark curly hair and olive complexion.

My legs are toned and long, and my hips curve out and then pinch in at the waistline.

The pads of my fingers stroke over a small scar, no bigger than an inch, on the right side of my stomach.

Daughter recovering in hospital from a stab wound to the abdomen.

The only mother I remember is my adoptive mom.

She was always attentive and patient with me. She spoiled me with clothes and trips abroad.

Her love was shown in her attendance to every school function, and the photos she insisted on taking to document my existence in this world. She would offer to wash my hair in the bath and always laid out my nightwear on the bed for me.

She read to me before I went to sleep and taught me about being a woman.

She was loving and caring, always offering comfort when girls were cruel to me in high school.

The thought of her being capable of harming me was absurd, so how much must my birth mother have hated me, us, our family, to resort to such drastic measures?

Garret would tell me that she went through a breakdown that affected her brain and caused her to lose herself. I can almost hearing him saying it, like we've already had the conversation, and that too faded and got lost inside my brain.

I don't understand who or what she was, and it leaves

me needing to fill in that void.

My gaze lifts back to the mirror.

My skin stretches over my ribcage, little rivets in my skin like waves on an ocean. All the swimming keeps me lean; my breasts sit perky on my chest, the dark pink nipples erect.

I follow the thick curls that hang down my back, turning to study the back of my body. Scars in different shades and sizes display across my back like a blow art painting; the ones you do in kindergarten, where they cut a straw, dip it in paint and make you blow through to create "art".

My spine chases down to my ass, the cheeks firm and pronounced. They hide forgotten sin. I know if I were to spread the cheeks, old, thick scarring around the hole would taunt me.

I was nine when I lost my memory. So whatever caused the scarring, or who, was lost. A blessing. A curse. Not remembering my life, even if it was horrible, is something that has shaped who I am.

Who am I?

I wish I didn't care, didn't need to know, but there is a constant nagging in my subconscious telling me I need to wake up. It's lonely and I feel constantly disengaged from everything and everyone around me. Who was I? What happened to me? Why don't I remember?

CHAPTER FIVE

IMP

The lake is calm and there's something floating on the surface.

Small, a doll maybe? I try to wade into the water but it turns to cement beneath me, not allowing me to save the doll… the person.

My mouth opens, calling out, but I can't hear the words.

"Evi," a small voice calls from the water, and my heart breaks, shattering into a mass of ashes.

The wind carries the dust over the water, and when it settles over the form in the water, my body crumbles.

A cold blast shocks me and my eyelids spring open just as I'm submerged into the lake. The cold mass consumes me, dragging me under. It's a rude awakening and causes my heart to almost stop completely.

You were sleepwalking.

Kicking my legs, I break the surface and gasp for air, coughing out the water that rushed into my mouth when I wasn't prepared for it. I'd been sleepwalking and must have been at the edge of the pier.

I'd been tired last night and didn't take a sleeping pill. Most nights they keep me dosed enough that I don't move from the bed.

My dreams are vivid but distorted. Just like my memories, they don't make sense to me.

Since I'm already in the water, I pull my nightshirt over my head and dump it on the small pier that leads to the water.

Pushing through the current, I lose myself to the strides forcing my body to fight the weight of the water, pushing myself.

The farther I swim out, the colder the water becomes.

I love how secluded this place is. With only the odd scattering of lake houses—eight in total—in the entire stretch of woodland, most are only occupied in the summer months and the rest of the year it's empty. Perfect.

As I reach the marker I always swim to so I have enough energy to swim back, I turn and make my way back.

Daylight brightens the sky and the birds sing to each other.

As I breach the pier line, a stone skits across the surface of the water and collides with my forehead.

My feet seek out the ground and I rush from the water to find Leroy standing on my land, staring at me.

"You must have seen me?" I bark. Anger coils my nerves.

Shrugging, he just stares at me, eyes wide and mouth slightly open.

My hand had instinctively gone to my head before I left the water, and as I remove it, watery blood coats my palm and I feel the warmth of it running down my face.

He blanches and walks toward me.

Holding my hand out to stop his approach, rage cooks in my veins.

"I didn't mean to get you," he says.

"Bullshit!" The blood coats my eyelashes and blurs my vision in one eye.

"Shit, you're really bleeding." His gawking keeps dropping to my chest, the pervert fuck.

"Go get your father, Leroy."

His face screws up into a scowl. "Oh, you'd like that, wouldn't you?"

"Yes." What a stupid question.

Blood is now dripping off my chin and down my body. I look down to realize I'd taken off the nightshirt and was swimming in just panties.

No wonder this shit face's eyes nearly bugged out of his skull. The only other tits he's probably seen are his mother's when he was breastfeeding.

"I saw him, you know?"

Walking up the pier, I pick up the wet shirt and hold it to the bleeding wound.

"Saw who, Leroy?" If this wound scars, I'm going to give him a matching one, the little brat.

"My dad leaving your house last night all flustered."

The snoop. I knew he'd be out here, lurking.

He needed a therapist. Maybe I'd give Garret's card.

"Were you spying on me again, you pervert?"

He squints and his lip lifts in a sneer.

"No. Don't flatter yourself."

I laugh. It's spontaneous and loud. "Is that why you hit me with a stone? Because you think I'm fucking your father? Jealous little boy, Leroy?"

"Fuck, no. He's old and cheating on my goddamn mother."

Rolling my shoulder, sick of his jealous outburst, I bite down on my anger.

"He was fixing a cut for me, you idiot child. Now, go get your dad or I'm going to call the police and have you arrested for assault."

His eyes bulge and his neck flares with a red rash.

"It was an accident."

"No, it wasn't, and we both know it."

He stares at me for a solid five seconds before gritting his teeth and running to get his father.

I make it inside and collapse onto the couch, the throbbing pain familiar and welcome.

I'm going to have this couch steam cleaned; the blood coats the cushion covers and clots in my hair.

My skin prickles with a sprinkle of cold awareness, the fabric under my bare thigh itching my skin.

I'm always sensitive after a swim, my body humming

with awareness of every nerve ending, the hot blood racing through every vein like a fever. Taste, touch, and hearing; everything felt heightened.

"Evi?"

Edward's cautious tone penetrates my ears, causing my lids to flutter open.

My gaze is unfocused and the room spins a little.

"What happened to you?" He rushes to my side, scanning over my body for injury. Leroy has joined him and is openly staring at my tits.

Soak it up, you little freak.

"Get out, Leroy!" I demand.

His father's stare shoots to his son and then back to me as if noticing for the first time that I'm almost naked.

Grabbing a throw pillow to cover me, he nods over to his son, gesturing him to leave.

Huffing like a five-year-old, Leroy says, "Whatever," over his shoulder, slamming my front door behind him as he leaves.

Edward takes the nightshirt that I still had over my head, and I hug the pillow he placed in my lap and watch his worried regard and fallen brow as he inspects the cut.

"What happened?"

Peeling my lips apart, I grunt. "Your son was skipping stones."

His gaze focuses on mine, the lines around his features more visible in daylight. "He did this?"

I pull my gaze from his. "It was an accident," I lie, knowing Leroy deserves more than his father's wrath. Revenge is better served from the source of their jealousy.

"You're ice cold." He places the back of his hand against my cheek. The contrast of his warmth against the cold of my flesh makes his hand feel like a flame against me.

"I was swimming."

Taking his hand away, he gestures to the wound.

"It's stopped bleeding and I can use some medical glue so it hopefully won't scar."

The blue material of Leroy's sweater passes the window behind Edward and my insides ignite.

Fuck you, Leroy.

"Evi, about last night…"

Before he can finish the sentence, I launch forward, getting up and straddling his lap, throwing the cushion to the floor as I do.

His hands clumsily catch me and his mouth pops open in surprise.

My bare chest pushes against the cotton of his t-shirt, my arms wrapping around his neck.

The burn of his palms around my back signal that he's not going to deny me.

Of course he isn't.

Dry blood tightens the skin on my face but it doesn't appear to bother Edward.

His cock grows thick beneath my pussy, which grinds into him.

I cup his face and pull his lips down to my neck so I can see around him to his jealous son, glaring at me through the window.

I grin wickedly back at him and lean back farther,

letting the good doctor kiss down my chest and suck a nipple into his greedy mouth.

The figure at the window disappears and I push Edward back. He's panting heavily and his fixated gaze is full of turmoil.

"I think I need to lie down," I murmur, and he snaps back into doctor/patient mode.

Moving me from his lap, he goes about cleaning me up and patching the wound.

I close my eyelids and pretend to fall asleep, waiting for the clicking of the front door as he leaves before I sit back up.

Images pass by the window again and I jolt to my feet, knocking the box that contains my other life to the floor as I do.

The contents splay out across the floor, a documented sadness of the true evil that can be in anyone.

Picking up a handwritten letter with a stamp from federal prison on the top, my heartbeat stampedes a million miles a minute.

My body collapses to a sitting position on top of the table.

There's a tremble in my hands as I drop to my knees and crawl to retrieve it.

Dear Evi,

This is one of the hardest things I have ever had to do.
    I hope by the time you're reading this,

you've had enough time to heal from the events of your life with us.

I know this will be hard for you to hear, but I do love you. Back when you were a little girl, I was also only a young girl and did some stupid things. Your father was an enigma to me, and mixed with the drugs, he ruled my life. Because of that, I didn't do what I should have to protect you from us. I hope you have forgiven me now.

I will be released by the time you receive this letter, but I won't come looking for you. I want you to live your life with hope and peace. Your grandma (my mother) left you the house in her will. If you can't face going back there you can sell it on and never think about that place and what happened there again.

Just know I don't regret what I did, only that I didn't take action sooner.

Thinking of you always,
Mom

Tossing the letter away from my body as if it was on fire, a pit opens in my chest.

How can she not regret what she did? The phantom pain of the stab wound hums on my abdomen. I search the pile of paper and find a deed with my name printed on it. Keys still sit in the overturned box.

Thoughts mull around, not finding root, only expanding further questions.

Why would she be released?
Why would I be left the house?
Where would she go?
Do I want to go back there?

CHAPTER SIX

DIJAN

Throwing some clothes and a toothbrush into my suitcase, I lock up the lake house and walk over to Edward's place.

His wife, Jacqueline, is standing on their porch, wrapped in a blanket and staring into the distance. Lost.

"Hey," I say timidly.

Seeing her standing there makes her a real person who I completely disregarded when I'd played games with Leroy and Edward earlier.

Her tired eyes rimmed with dark circles drop to where I'm standing at the bottom of the stairs from their house.

"Oh, Evi. Hey." She speaks with a slur, her tone mixed

with confusion.

"How are you, Jacqueline?" I know it's a stupid question. It was one I hated when people asked me constantly after I woke up and didn't remember anything.

No. I'm not okay.

"Have you seen Daniel?"

She asks but I think she means Leroy and I don't have the heart to correct her.

"No."

"I saw you swimming. Daniel is a good swimmer, don't believe what they tell you Evi," she states, shaking her head and looking out over the water.

He wasn't a good swimmer, he was an ok swimmer at best.

"I used to love it up here. Been coming since I was little," she murmurs, pulling the blanket further around her body.

"How are you? Both those boys are so fond of you. Were." She frowns.

Another misconception on her part. Leroy wasn't fond of me. He had a fascination and a deep-seated anger toward me.

The door opens behind her and Edward steps out, his jaw tense, every muscle straining.

"Evi." He says my name in warning. "What are you doing with a suitcase?" He places an arm around Jacqueline. She doesn't react. It's almost like she's vacant from her body.

"I was going to ask if you would give me a ride into town."

Dropping his arm from Jacqueline, he walks down the steps.

"Are you leaving?" Concern etches across his features and my stare darts back up to his wife, who isn't paying us any attention.

He follows my stare and scoffs, taking me by the arm and walking a few more yards away.

"Don't worry about Jacqueline. She's on enough medication that anything she hears or sees can be explained as a dream."

I want to question him on that more; he's never been so dismissive or cold toward her before, but it's none of my business and I have enough to think about without adding their issues to the pile.

"I'm just visiting some family for a few days."

Lies.

"Is this because of what happened?"

Oh God. He's deluded to think that would cause me to flee.

"No, of course not. Nothing even happened, Edward." I fold my arms and kick at the dirt.

"I'll be home in a few days. Can you take me or not?"

He studies me, placing a hand on his hip and scrubbing along his chin with the other hand.

"Sure. Give me five minutes to get Jacqueline settled in the house."

The ride is quiet and uncomfortable. Edward keeps looking

over at me and my mind is on the phone conversation I had with Garret before I left.

"I'm going to go to the house. Maybe it will help with my memories."

"I think that's a good idea. It can stimulate familiarity, but you shouldn't go alone, Evi. It may also cause stress and trauma. You could regress further into yourself."

The anxiety eats away at me like tiny bugs crawling around under the skin, devouring until there's nothing but frayed nerves left.

"Then come with me. I need you, Garret."

His heavy sigh down the line rumbles and crackles the signal. "If you give me a few days, maybe I can…"

More excuses.

"It's okay. We can talk about it more later," I say and end the call.

The town is really a couple of shops, a post office, and a train station. It's quant and has been run by the same family for decades.

Edward pulls into a space and the tension becomes unbearable.

"So, I'll see you in a few days," I tell him, unlocking the door and stepping out into the light rain.

He follows suit and my heart sinks. I wish he would have just stayed in the car. I feel dirty and awkward in his presence all of a sudden and I wish I'd just walked here.

Opening the trunk, he pulls my suitcase out. "Do you want me to wait with you?"

"No," I snap too quickly, and I recoil when he jerks his head to mine and pins me with a stare that looks too deeply within me.

"Thank you for bringing me, but it's fine. You can get back to your wife. Jacqueline." I stumble over my words and it all feels odd and out of place.

We don't fit and everyone knows it.

"Have a safe trip then," he says, cautiously eyeballing me over the hood. I nod my head in response and wave half-heartedly.

This is it. I'm going back to the beginning.

The unsettled stirring of my stomach is in full-blown tornado force as I step from the cab on the street I grew up on. Familiarity invades my senses and my mind tells me to run.

The storm closes in around me, almost in warning of what this place is, and yet I know I can't run. I need to face this to be able to move on with my life.

After discussing whether or not to come here with Garret, he texted me an hour ago, offering to accompany me, but it would need to be next week. I told him I would wait but was already on the train traveling here.

The keys dangle from my finger and my feet stick to the pavement as if the cement is wet and I'm sinking into it, to be its prisoner forever.

"There you go," the driver says, planting my suitcase next to me.

The lights from him pulling away fade, along with my chance to turn back.

Night has crept up on me, blanketing the street in a haunting darkness. A street light flickers a few feet away and I find my arms wrapping around my torso in a hug to protect myself from whatever this place holds.

There are lots of houses boarded up and derelict, yet the garden of the house I now own has been kept trimmed and the shutters have a fresh coat of paint.

The house next door is lived in; a small sliver of light seeps out from drawn drapes.

Their house is well-kept, as is their neighbor's, but that's where the tidy row ends.

Overgrown, graffiti-adorned boards covering window holes on the other houses make it look like a forgotten place. *Ironic.*

A chill races up my spine as a glimmer of a memory sparks.

It's sunny. The street is full of people sitting in deckchairs in their gardens, and kids racing around shooting water guns. I feel myself, the old me, standing on the sidewalk. Everyone stops moving as if frozen in time and all attention is on me. Sad gawks, staring at me in pity.

"Hey, you."

A croaky voice pierces the night and draws me back to the now. I was lost in a memory. I hadn't even realized how detailed it was and how swallowed by it I'd become.

Maybe Garret was right and this place will unlock more of my past life.

The neighbor from the tidy house next to mine has come out onto her porch.

Skin hangs from her bones, wrinkled. Grey hair

droops in stringy strands. Her hunched shoulders make her appear short.

"This isn't a sightseeing attraction. Get gone." She waves a walking stick in the air to drive her point home.

Oh, scary.

I open the gate to my house. It rattles and scrapes over the concrete path. I cringe internally at the sound and march up to the house without looking at the old lady.

"Hey! Did you not hear what I said? I'll call my son."

Oh God. She lives here with her son. The wrinkles littering her skin show she must be in her seventies at least.

Who lives with their mom when she's seventy? He must be a real treat. Forty-year-old virgin pops into my mind, and I snort, jamming the keys into the lock and opening the door as fast as I can, disappearing through it and slamming it shut.

Thud...

I'm facing the door, and all of a sudden it dawns on me that I've shut myself in a house that holds ghosts, and I'm not sure if I'm ready to face them.

Night time has plunged everything into darkness and I scramble to pull my cell phone from my pocket and bring up the torch app, using it as a light source to locate the actual light switch.

I didn't even think that someone could be in here. What if my mother lives here and used the deed as a ploy to get me to come here so she can finish the job?

My ears prick to listen for movement but it's still and quiet. Too damn quiet.

My fingers brush over the wall next to me as I take

tentative steps forward, searching for a light.

When my hand hits the switch sticking out from the wall, I exhale in relief, only to gasp when nothing happens.

Flick, flick, flick. Nothing.

Damn it.

The power is out and I should have known that by just doing the math of how long this house had been empty, waiting for me to come of age. My stomach somersaults, making sickness stir.

I can't stay here in the pitch black; there's a stagnant thickness in the air making me want to gag.

The shadows taunt me, every corner deep and dark like a black abyss, and every object a threat of being so much more.

Moonlight pours through a window and highlights a doorway into the kitchen.

There may be candles.

Shuffling my feet forward, I go to the kitchen and use the natural light to search the drawers and cabinets, only to find nothing.

There's an earthy smell emitting from some of the cupboards but I can't see that there is anything within them that could be creating the smell.

I can't stay here.

Cold damp creeps into my bones and an overwhelming feeling seeps into my heart. I will myself not to cry, not understanding why my body wants to do just that.

Emotion I've never experienced before crashes over me. It overcomes me like a wave engulfing me in a once calm sea, unprepared for it.

I didn't see it coming until it was towing me under and sweeping me away in its current.

My mouth opens and I want to scream, but a weird, empty sound comes from the gaping hole instead.

My bones feel like they're cracking and snapping, caving in on themselves to crush the organs beneath. Tears burn and leak freely down my face like a torrential downfall. My legs give out on me and I crumble to the floor, my knees making a nasty thud as I land. Curling into myself, I lie there and cry years and years of pain out onto the kitchen floor of a house I spent nine years growing up in.

It's too much. I can't contain it.

Garret warned me of this happening. The magnitude of coming back here could cause a break in my psychological healing. Well, fuck you, Garret for never being here when I truly need you.

My eyes close to ease the exhaustion of the sobs ripping out of me. All I want to do is close my mind off and wake up remembering who I am so I can heal and move on from this nightmare.

CHAPTER SEVEN

BEAST

Something is tickling my face. If that freak has crept in here again to watch me sleep, I'm going to kill him. My body jolts with awareness and I quickly swipe at my cheek and shoot up to my feet, wincing when my knees protest the action. A fat-bodied spider scuttles across the tiled floor.

Gross.

I stamp my foot down on the offender.

And remember where I am.

The kitchen is bathed in sunlight now and it highlights the utter filth I slept on.

Black, thick grime is everywhere, mold crawling up

the walls like spreading ink spilt over paper, making me gag. The smell is rancid, invading my nostrils and clinging to the back of my throat. Rushing to the back entrance, I open the door with a hip nudge and spill into the yard. It wasn't even locked.

Anyone could have been in here.

Thud...

My heart stampedes when flashes of me looking down at my abdomen and seeing a blade sticking from it assault me.

Blood. Cold rain. Fuzzy thoughts. I'm small and fragile and swallowing down pain as my mouth mumbles words to someone.

"I called my son. He's coming right over," a voice croaks, disintegrating the memory I was just fixated within.

I look up at the window of the neighbor to see her sticking her head from it and scowling at me.

Fall, you old hag.

Crazy old bat. So, her son doesn't live there, and if he doesn't live with her, why would he allow her to live in such an abandoned part of town?

Maybe she's mentally ill and doesn't even have a son.

I wave goodbye to her, more of a taunt than being polite, and go back inside. The deep-rooted need to swim plants itself like a virus, itching my skin.

I turn on the kitchen tap and it chugs and splats before clean running water pours free. Cupping my hands under the flow, I take handfuls and splash my face over and over. The cold blast feels so good, I just want to shrink and dive into it.

Inhaling deeply, I open my eyes and startle when a pair of dark orbs stare back at me through the glass. Turning the tap off, I back away from the window with caution until my ass bumps against a fridge.

The intruder moves to the back door. His full frame takes up the entire space of the doorway.

"What the hell are you doing in there? You're trespassing." Authority and hostile aggression pours from him in waves; it's almost visible as a separate entity.

My head is shaking from side to side and I find myself grasping the keys from the counter and holding them up to him as proof that I'm allowed to be here.

His brows knit together as he studies me through the dirt-stained glass. Goosebumps sprout all over my flesh when he drags his regard up my body, beginning at my feet. His features pinch. Nervous flurries awake in my stomach as I take in his appearance.

He's wearing black, heavy boots. His long, muscular legs stretch up, with jeans sitting loosely on his narrowed hips. His t-shirt is white and sticks to his upper body like a second skin, only gaining loose fabric around his midriff. Tattooed arms with veins bulging rest against the door as he leans in to see me through the pane of glass. Brown strands of thick hair sit on top of his head. He has dark, penetrating spheres cased in a half moon of thick dark lashes, and a slim nose. Plump, generous lips part, and his chiseled bone structure shapes high cheekbones and a square jaw. His chest begins to inflate and deflate rapidly.

"It can't be," he breathes, causing the glass to mist. "No. You were gone. You need to stay gone," he whispers, his brow furrowed and frown lines etching over his beautiful face.

I always thought Garret was the best-looking man I'd ever seen but this stranger before me was something else entirely.

What the hell was he talking about again?

"Why would you come back here?" he demands, and my insides have bottomed out. I feel light-headed and ready to pass out.

Does he know who I am?

"Evi?" he continues, and my heart thuds so out of sync that the room spins around me, almost as if I'm stepping out of myself.

The name's Max. I just moved into the house back there. What's there to do around here?

The flash of memory is gone as quickly as it appeared.

A small gush of air wisps my hair and coats my skin in awareness that he's opened the door. He steps inside, making the room appear to shrink around his size. "Are you going to answer me?"

"I don't know you."

His nostrils flare and then he laughs, loud and boisterous. "It's Max, Evi. Jesus." His gaze narrows and his hands go to his hips. "From next door. Are you serious right now?"

"I lost my memory."

Even if I hadn't, I was only nine when I lived here. It wouldn't be that much of a surprise if I didn't remember him, even with my memories intact. He would have been just a boy and now he's a mammoth. He looks like a lumberjack.

His focus is zoned in on me, assessing. I hate that look; Garret gives me the same one.

Are you crazy?

"Why are you here?" he asks, ignoring my admission.

My hands fidget, his domineering presence stirring a little fear, but worse than that, I can feel my body responding to the fear. I like it.

"I own this house."

"This isn't a house, it's a tomb, and it should have been torn down years ago. Why would you want to come back here?"

He sounds disgusted; that me being curious, me being here makes me sick or something. Well, I am sick. Sick of not knowing what the hell happened to me and who my family was before I was adopted and given a new one.

"I want answers. I closed my eyes twelve years ago in this yard and woke up on the wrong side of reality," I tell him, more honest than I've ever been with anyone else.

Shaking his head, ghosts haunt his eyes as he stares at me. "No, Evi. That life should be forgotten. It's a blessing that you don't remember." He takes a step backward, almost protecting me from his presence. Like maybe his aura so close to mine could evoke those memories back to me.

My hand moves to the scar on my stomach and I know I shouldn't want to remember, but I do. It's like losing someone. You can never truly heal from it; you just go on living with them haunting you.

"What do you know about me, about my life then?" I urge, suddenly hopeful.

This is the first time I've met another person who knew the old me. We were young, but we knew each other. He knows who I am.

Darkness shrouds him like a shadow, blotting out the sun in the room.

"I was your neighbor," he says, quiet and guarded.

I already know that. Tell me more.

"Were you friends with my brothers?" It would make sense.

His face contorts as if he tasted something disgusting on his tongue. "No. I hated those assholes. I was your friend."

I can't explain it, but I already knew that answer. Something inside me wants to go to him and hug him, something buried in my soul pulling me toward him like a magnetic force, summoning me.

The way he said *hated* with such ferocity and passion causes a pulse to drum in my neck. Why did he hate them and say he was my friend like my brothers and I were enemies?

"Do you still live here?" I ask.

His shoulders drop, and the tick in his jaw from moments before dissipates. "No. My mom does because she refuses to move so I spend time here looking after her and the house." He shrugs, a pretty pink tinge highlighting his cheeks.

I look out at the yard, and its cleanliness compared to the inside of the house. "Are you the one taking care of the gardens?"

His gaze follows mine and he shrugs. "I do both sides

so my mother doesn't have to look at an overgrown mess. No one has been here in years."

Moving his focus to a spot on the concrete just below the window, the room temperature shifts, and all of a sudden, I feel freezing cold, despite the sun beaming through the window and heating the space like an oven.

His head drops to his shoes, and when he looks back up, my stomach twists with the force of the raw emotion shining back at me through his dark, penetrating orbs.

"I tried to visit you in the hospital and they wouldn't let me and then you were just gone. I looked for you, but you disappeared."

Grief, fresh and turbulent, laces his tone, and his locked jaw flexing with deep swallows shields his face like armor.

My feet take a step in his direction without permission. "I was adopted." The words whispering from my lips are almost in apology.

"And you forgot about me," he murmurs, more to himself then to me.

"I forgot *me*," I whisper back.

Before I can prepare myself, he closes the gap between us with a few short strides, his huge frame encompassing my much smaller one, lifting me clear from the floor into a bear hug, his mouth to my ear, his arms around my waist so tight it almost steals my breath from my lungs. It's awkward and unexpected, but my arms find his neck, wrapping around and clinging on for dear life. Something shifts inside me, a relaxing peace dousing me. Usually, only swimming can bring me that emotion.

"I can't believe it's really you." He exhales against the skin just below my ear.

My lids close and I breathe in his earthy scent. It feels nice being in someone's arms. Someone who appears to have genuine sentiment toward me.

He puts me back on my feet and pulls away, shaking his head and running his hand through his hair, creating the tussles to shoot off in all directions.

"I'm sorry I did that. It must be weird for you." He gestures with his hands, pointing to me and then letting his arm fall, the palm of his hand slapping against his thigh as he does. "So, you honestly don't remember anything at all?" His brow quirks.

Folding my arms around myself, I shrug. "I woke in the hospital with a stab wound and didn't know anything. Not even my name."

His focus drops to my abdomen where the small scar burns with phantom memories. A sensation of rain hitting my face pours over me. It's so vivid my gaze lifts to the ceiling to check there isn't a leak.

"This place is a mess. You shouldn't be in here."

There's no leak, and I know the droplets I felt moments ago weren't real. Focusing back on the man before me, Max, I ask, "Can you tell me anything about myself?"

He shifts, uncomfortable at my line of questioning, anger flaring his nostrils. The storm brewing in his orbs makes me want to take shelter somewhere. "You liked to swim."

A sigh whispers from my lips. Contentment and joy flood my system. "I still do."

"I should get back and check on Mom. She'll be worried."

"Okay," I tell him, but a pit opens in my chest at the thought of being left alone in this house.

"Bye." He's out the door before I can respond.

I want to ask him to stay or come back later, but his strides are huge and he's gone before I can even think.

CHAPTER EIGHT

HELLION

The smell, pungent and suffocating, overwhelms me when I open the cupboards to see if there's anything inside. They're empty apart from moss.

This place should have been condemned; it's gross.

My feet carry me through to the living room; old furniture lays askew at weird angles as if it had been pushed out of the way and just left abandoned in a hurry. There's dirt thick on all the surfaces and a stream of dust particles swirl in the light streaming through the window, making me want to sneeze and cover my face with a surgical mask all in the same breath.

I will my memory to give me something, to stir any

recollection, but nothing comes.

My cell phone vibrates and Garret's name pops up on the screen. I don't answer it. The battery beeps to warn me it's about to die.

Perfect. I'm here with nowhere to charge it.

Slipping the phone back in my pocket, I make my way through the house and come to a closed door just down the corridor to the left of the living room. My hand hovers at the handle, trepidation triggering my movement to slow as I push it down and the metal clicks. Dread cramps my stomach, almost buckling me over in pain. Fear, fresh and real, almost like falling and not knowing if you're going to be able to catch yourself, swarms me like bees pushing their stings into my pores. Darkness clouds in around me, despite it being morning. An emotional storm crackles the atmosphere around me.

Thud...

Pushing the door open, it squeals with the effort and expands the inside with every inch it cracks open.

Thud...

A stench much worse than the one everywhere else hits me in the face like a fog. Sickness burns up my esophagus, threatening to spill over the floor.

What the hell is that?

Dead flies litter the worn carpet in dark heaps, like they all committed suicide in a pact. There are two twin beds situated on separate sides of the wall, mattresses bare of sheets and laid askew, half on and half off the base, sullied with dark stains. Placing a hand over my mouth, my feet move forward but my lungs struggle, fighting for clean air.

I take another step inside and phantom screams echo around me.

"No! Please!"

"Don't!"

"No!"

The stains are blood. Flickers of images spin in my mind. Crimson puddles. Crying. Screams. Cuts. Pain.

Teen boys laughing and sneering before their screams are all there is and then it's gone as quick as it came, a passing thunderstorm leaving me shaking in its wake. Itching need shoots through my veins to flee and my feet move without command. Before I can recall leaving the room, I'm outside, gagging and dropping to my knees. The concrete scrapes over my skin, but it doesn't matter. The fresh air filling my lungs brings my nerves under control as I expel the last of the acid in my guts over the floor.

Trees, tall and billowing, sway in the steady breeze, the whooshing sounds of their leaves mimic the sound of waves and it calls to me.

I'm okay.

There's an old wooden fence, discolored and patched with old mismatched panels. A rickety old gate sways, cracking like thunder every now and then when the breeze picks it up and slams it shut. Getting to my feet, a hiss whizzes past my lips as the sting on my knees makes itself known.

I open the back gate and my breath stills at the scenery.

There are trees and dirt paths going in all directions. It's beautiful and reminds me of the lake house. It's like a hidden world tucked behind a horror show.

Following one of the paths, I let instinct guide my feet, picking up the pace and enjoying the heavy thump of my heart, dutifully reminding me I'm alive. Having no cell phone and no power to charge it eats away at my thoughts the farther I walk, and I know I need to do something about that or find a hotel to stay in for the night. A hot shower and a meal sound appealing right about now.

I debate turning back. I've been wandering without consequence of the distance I've walked for a good thirty minutes, but I push the urge to the back of my mind to get lost with so much already hidden here.

Barking snaps into the air, alerting me to the presence of a dog that bounds from some brush and shakes his body manically, sending water drops flying in all direction, including up my legs.

A voice calls out for him to wait. "Rocko!"

A woman appears a second later and she startles when she sees me standing there. Her hand reaches for her chest, her face paling at the sight of me. "Oh, Lord. You gave me a fright."

"Sorry."

Her black Labrador drops a ball at my feet and she rolls her eyes. "Not everyone wants to play with you, Rocko. Sorry. He's not used to seeing people on our walks."

His wet fur brushes against my leg so I reach down to pet him. "He's all wet."

The woman takes the few steps toward, me closing the space. She looks to be in her late fifties; crinkles decorate her face, showing her life experience like a road map for all to see. Her cotton tee has mud spatter and she's wearing rain boots.

"He goes in the lake. It's hard to keep him from it."

My head snaps up to her face. "Lake?"

She nods over her shoulder and studies me for a few silent beats. "Yes. Just through the trees. I wouldn't recommend going down there by yourself."

My brow pinches at her words. "Why?"

Her brow mimics mine. "Are you staying around here?" she asks abruptly.

Folding my arms over my chest, I kick the tennis ball at my feet away and watch Rocko go fetch it.

"Yes. Why?" My tone is defensive, and rightly so. I don't like being interrogated by strangers acting weird and like they own the place.

"It's just I haven't seen you before and…" She looks around. "I know pretty much everyone who still lives around here." Maybe she's just protective of where she lives; I can relate to that. Up at the lake house we're on alert when strangers appear, just in case they're camping in the woods without permission and might cause trouble, leave litter, or burn fires incorrectly.

"It's so pretty here. Why did people move away?" I query, ignoring her question, astounded that such a place could be abandoned and left to the wild.

Brushing down her shorts, she shakes her head and then moves to a fallen tree stump and sits, absentmindedly tugging the tennis ball from her dog's mouth and tossing it into the thicket.

"When the plans for the shopping mall got scrapped

and the plant closed, it forced many people to move on. It was a pretty new area built for the workers of the plant, so when it closed, there was no need for people to stay around here." She shrugs, looking down and scraping some mud from her boot using the heel of the other one.

It's only about an hour from the local town though; surely people could travel from here into the town? It seems like such a waste.

She's watching me like she can read my thoughts.

"Superstition is a powerful thing, and also played a part in why people didn't stick around. It's a small community. You must have heard the rumors about this place if you're staying with someone here?"

It's a question again, prying to find out who I'm here with. A shiver rakes over my skin. "Superstition? About the Devil family murder, you mean?"

Her eyes narrow and my heart stampedes in my chest. Will she know who I am? Does it show on my face? Do I look like them?

Irrational. Calm down, Evi.

"They were a cult family. Used to worship the devil and make sacrifices in the woods. They cursed this place, the crazy mother killing those children as an offering. Absolute insanity, and people didn't want to be near the cursed house or lake."

Cult?

Offering?

What the hell?

"The lake?" I ask, ignoring her other comments. I get people not wanting to live next to a murder scene, but why the lake?

She nods once again through the brush and swipes at a stray tear. "Awful. So young."

"Who?"

Rocko begins barking insistently at footfalls sounding from the direction I came from. The woman gets to her feet. "Rocko, come here."

Through a small clearing, Max comes into view.

No feature stands out above the rest on his beautiful face, each one as perfect as the next. His eyes hold an intensity like none I've witnessed before and his dark orbs make him even more appealing, hiding secrets within them. It's not just the color though; in any shade they would be unflawed. It's the almond shape and the way all his emotions display there like a projector screen.

"Oh, Maxwell." She beams. "Is this the friend you're here with?" she asks me curiously, giving me a knowing crinkle of her eyes.

Wringing my hands together, I don't know what to say. I want to say yes but I don't want to put him on the spot, and I don't want him telling her who I really am. The way she spoke of my family, such animosity, not just towards my mother who committed the crime but towards them as an entirety.

Was I like them? Did I do the things she speaks of?

"Gertrude." Max nods his head and kneels to stroke and play with the dog.

"I was just asking if you were the friend this young lady is staying with?" she asks, winking her eye but it looks odd like something flew in it.

"Always looking for gossip, Gertrude," he jests, giving her a wink, which makes the corners of her lips stretch over her face, reaching all the way up to her eyes. They are a diluted blue color and barren of any eyelashes.

"I'm getting old now, Maxwell. I must live vicariously through the younger generation."

Standing to his full height, he comes to stand beside me, nudging me with his arm. "You don't look a day over thirty," he says, initiating a cackle from her lips

"Well, I wouldn't go that far but there is plenty of spirit in me, yet" She points towards him, a sultry tinge to her tone.

My eyes widen and I have to bite on my gum to stop from smirking.

"I should get Rocko home. Don't forget to stop by so I can pay you for moving that trash for me," she tells Max, and puts Rocko's lead in place, waving her hand in the air as she leaves us standing there.

Bugs whizz and hum around us, floating like feathers after a pillow fight, and the sun is shining only we're hidden beneath the canopy of the trees, making it appear much cooler than it is. The small streams of sunlight that penetrate through the branches glitter and sparkle, making it ethereal.

I'm aware of how close Max is standing to me on a level I don't want to explore; I wish the need inside me wasn't so dominating at times. Hiding the demons inside only lasts so long.

"What are you doing out here?" he asks, shattering the silence. His body turns into mine, and he's so close his scent wraps around mc like a blanket, touching every folli-cle standing in awareness over my skin.

He's so much taller than me. I find myself staring at his chest and wondering if he's hairless under his top or if he has a dusting of hair like a grizzly bear ready to eat me up.

"I needed some fresh air. It's stunning back here," I whisper, quelling the impure thoughts with a squeeze of my thighs.

Looking over at where Gertrude said the water is, I ponder how large the lake is. How deep, how cold and freeing.

His chest moves up and down with his breathing but he's not saying anything. Slowly, I creep my eyes up his body to see him once again examining me intently.

"I don't think you should be out here, especially alone."

A snort rumbles out of me, quickly followed by a crim-son splattering of embarrassment. "Because of the devil worshipping and offerings?"

Rolling his eyes, he reaches out and rubs down my arm and I feel it all the way down to the marrow of my bones. "Is that what Gertrude was telling you? She's an old fruit loop, Evi. Been around here way too long with no life so she embellishes the truth."

I move towards the brush but I'm stopped by his hand grabbing me, halting me. He's so strong; there's no strain or effort in his actions.

"Where are you going?"

I stare at his plump lips and lose myself to them and how fat they are. If I bit into them, would they pop like the skin on a peach?

"Down to the water." I pull my arm free and jog forward.

"Evi," he warns, but I ignore him and push towards where Gertrude had been gesturing. My feet stumble to a stop after clearing the trees when the water comes into view.

Lake?

It's more of a pond than a lake, the dark green color off-putting with swirls of dirt and oil sitting on the surface. There's no movement, no waves. It lays dormant.

Disappointment and something else I can't pinpoint seeps inside me.

"Why didn't you want me seeing this? It's pathetic." I shrug, rubbing my chest where an incessant thud pounds, keeping me alive.

He's just watching me again and I shrink under his scrutiny. What response was he expecting? I'm at such a disadvantage when it comes to him.

"Max! Tell me why you were so against me coming here?"

He moves towards me and points off towards a rocky area. "A boy was murdered over there it was around the same time as your family."

I follow his line of sight and then look back at him.

That's awful, but so what?

"What happened to him?" He doesn't speak and I want to scream at him and pound my fist against his huge chest. "Just tell me, goddamn it!" I demand, sick of this tiptoeing. I'm not a child.

"They say your mother murdered him and buried him

in the woods."

They say your mother murdered him.

The empty hole that lives inside my chest opens at his confession. Who the hell was this woman?

"Who is *they*?" I ask, confused. If it's stupid Gertrude then who knows what really happened.

"The police."

"Why? Who was he and why kill him here and go to the effort of burying him only to then go to the house and murder her entire family, unless it's what triggered her to actually want to kill everyone," I rush out. Spending too much time in Garret's sessions has given me an overactive imagination.

"It wasn't the same night"

My thoughts clash and collide and then stop. "What?"

"His remains were discovered around the same time as your families bodies, they searched the back area of your house and found a fresh-ish gravesite with his remains buried there but he had been killed weeks before."

My legs weaken and I drop to my butt, needing to sit before falling.

We weren't her only victims?

"Who was he?"

I sense his body moving towards me before his shadow casts me in shade. "He was a friend of your brother's."

A shiver passes through me, sending chills up my spine, and all the hairs stand on end on the back of my neck.

"Why did it take so long for them to find him? Did anyone report him missing?" I breathe, desperate for answers so everything makes some kind of sense.

"He was a troubled teen. His mom thought he ran away."

So she didn't look for him? How bad was he?

"Why would my birth mom do something like that?" It's not really a question for him, just one I want the answer to. Not knowing why is the worst part. I wish she left an address for me to find her so I can just get the answers from the source.

Why would she ever be allowed free?

Dropping down beside me, he shakes his head.

"Evi, don't lose sleep over him. He wasn't a good person."

I dart my eyes to his. "He was a kid, you said?"

"Sixteen. And a mean little asshole."

Exhaling, I close my eyes and try to think of the brothers I know I had, but nothing manifests and I'm left even more frustrated.

"What was my mother like?"

He becomes tense, snapping a blade of grass and pulling it between his fingers. "From what I remember about her, she was vacant."

"So, she wasn't around much?"

I can feel his eyes on the side of my face but I'm too frightened to look at him and see pity in his stare. "She was around, just high on meds"

High on meds?

"So, drugs?" I turn to face him, curious.

"Substance abuse is what they say led to her behavior."

"Who said that?"

"The policc. The papers. Theorists." He shrugs. "I was only twelve when it happened so I don't know everything." Irritation shows in his rigid posture and his constant pulling on the grass and flicking it towards the water.

"You said back at the house that you were my friend, not my brother's."

Sunlight bleeds through his hair making the strands shine with golden licks. His dark eyes melt to an almost caramel color when the sun catches them just right. A fever takes over my skin as I drink him in and the usual sense of shame follows the bad thoughts. I look back to the water and fight the urge to wade into it.

"I was younger than your brothers and didn't like them."

"Why?"

"They weren't good people. They weren't good to you. They should have looked after you and they didn't."

What if they needed to be looked after too? Why do I feel like he's not being truly forthcoming?

"You're being vague," I say.

"Because it's better for you that way."

Anger coils my muscles. How dare he say that? What the hell does he know? He knew me when I was nine. I'm a woman now and don't need anyone telling me what's best for me.

Getting to my feet, I leave him sitting there, watching me leave. The trees' stray branches brush past me as I pick up pace. Max's footfalls sound behind me and I know he's already caught up to me.

"Evi, don't be mad. I just don't think you'd want to

remember them."

Spinning, I push at his chest, poking my finger to make a point. "How dare you think for me? I'm a grown ass woman, Max. What do you think I came back here for? I need to know who I am, what happened to me. Them. Us."

Exhaustion overcomes me and my stomach growls. I haven't eaten since arriving, and even before that. My mouth is dry and making me trip on words. Loneliness leaks into me and I begin to feel like I don't exist at all. That maybe I died that day and all this is me in limbo.

"Evi, come have something to eat and rest for a while. That's what I was doing before coming out here. I came to find you when I noticed your gate open and you not there. Mom's made lunch."

The thought of food appeals over being grumpy and I find myself following him back to his mom's in silence, stomping my feet harder than necessary, just like the child I claimed I'm not anymore. The smirk on his lips tells me he finds it amusing, and for a second, the burden of not knowing anything lifts and all I want is to know him.

CHAPTER NINE

KNAVE

The aroma is enticing and water floods my mouth at the thought of eating whatever is in the pot Max's mother has placed on the table. She wanders in and out of the kitchen, bringing more items with her. Bread, vegetables, mashed potatoes, and a jug of iced tea.

"We don't get many visitors these days," she says, and guilt tickles up my spine. I'd wished her to fall out of her bedroom window when I thought she was being a pest, but she's just not used to having people around.

"Looks great, Mom," Max tells her, holding out her chair for her to sit down. He takes a tea towel from her hands and lifts the lid on the cooking pot. Steam carries the scent in the air and my stomach growls in response. Embarrassment lights my cheeks and Max chuckles. It's rich and from the soul and it makes my heart flutter inside my chest.

He offers me a ladle, grinning down at me, and takes the seat at the head with us either side of him on opposite sides of the table. "Help yourself, dear," his mom tells me.

And I do, scooping up a full spoonful of stew and adding all the trimmings. It's a full dinner, not just lunch, and as I shovel the first forkful into my mouth without waiting for them to even serve themselves some food, the blush deepens. I sigh as the warm food slides down and fills the empty space inside my gut. I need to eat more often instead of letting myself get so hungry. It's not good for my body or mind to not eat.

"So, Max tells me you inherited the house next door?"

Swallowing the food in my mouth, I nod, looking between Max and her, not knowing if he's told her who I am.

"Awful what happened there. I was never happy that Max befriended you."

Whack.

Her words puncture me like she's wielding a knife and not a tongue. I almost choke. Did I hear her right?

Silence hangs in the air and my feet fidget with the need to leave.

So, he has told her who I am. Why wouldn't she want him to be friends with me? I was an innocent nine-year-old.

"Mother," Max warns, but she looks perplexed and her small beady eyes fall over me.

"You used to always be down by that water, naked."

Naked?

At nine?

My appetite fades and mortification replaces it.

"She was a kid, Mother."

Scoffing, his mom waves her fork in my direction, her dewy, almost translucent skin looks like it could tear with her movements. "Old enough to know what's appropriate. Your mother was always showing off her body as well. My Graham saw more of her breasts than he did mine."

Whack.

I'm sure my mouth is agape, hanging on the hinges. My hand clenches into a fist and the urge to grab her and yank her across the table is so strong, my arm jerks.

"Mother!" Max pounds his fist down on the table causing us both to jolt in disbelief.

Excitement and turmoil spin and collide inside me, his tone and raw power making me drip between the thighs. I want him to rip down my panties and fuck me over this table right in front of his mother.

Oh, God. What the hell is wrong with me? I'm not normal. That's not normal.

"Evi."

I can hear him saying my name but it's so hard for me to focus on it and grasp onto reality. The bad thoughts are too strong. I'm envisioning his hard muscles beneath his clothes, his huge hands ripping my clothes to shreds in a frenzied state. Forcing me face down over the table, the food spilling to the floor and the wood grains scratching at my flesh as he kicks my ankles, spreading my legs and ramming me full of his hard, throbbing cock. His mother, mouth wide open, eyes as big as the plates now crashing to the floor.

Yeah. Fuck me, Max. Rough and raw. Cause friction hot enough to spark a flame. How inappropriate am I now, you old hag?

"Evi!" he yells, and I feel his hands on my arms, shaking me. My hold on the fantasy snaps and a fully dressed Max is shaking me in my seat. "Are you having a panic attack?" Concern glows in his eyes.

"No." My chest is heaving, my breathing labored. Jumping to my feet, I grab a napkin and swipe it across my lips. "Thank you for the food," I tell the beady eyes glaring at me.

"Please don't go. You hardly touched your food. Mom, Evi's family is off limits," Max growls, and she blinks up at him, all innocent and fragile.

"I meant no offense."

I want to poke her in the eye with her fork, and I will her to choke on the lump of meat she's cramming into her loose lips.

"Sit, Evi. Please," Max says.

Retaking my seat, I pick up the glass Max fills with iced tea and sip the liquid down, hoping it will fan the fire raging inside me.

"So, how old are you now, Evi?"

The atmosphere is temperamental and visions of me swimming back at the lake house make me miss being there.

"I've just turned twenty-one."

"Oh. Happy birthday to you then." She squints. Her

words arc bitter and I don't understand how my nine-year-old self could have offended her so much, unless it's just the sins of the mother.

"Thank you," I reply tightly.

"Are you in school?"

I shift in my seat, hating her questions. I'm not in school because I hate being around people. They irritate me. *Like her.*

"No, I'm not."

"So what do you do?"

"I own a lake house and spend most of my time there."

She frowns, producing creases on her forehead to overlap each other. She looks like an over-cooked chicken. "So what do you do for money?"

"Mother," Max cautions coolly.

Offering him a taut grin, I place my hand on his arm and embrace the energy fluttering in my chest when his mother's eyes zone in on my touch and her jaw goes rigid.

Oh, naughty Evi is touching your precious son.

"It's fine, Max. I coach swimming to kids at a nearby campsite where my lake house is. It's not a lot of money, but I don't need a lot, and my parents gifted me the house, so it's paid for."

Her crinkly brows iron out over her head when they drop low over her eyes. "Parents?" she scoffs, some food spitting from her mouth as she does.

Gross.

"I was adopted by a great couple when I was nine."

"My Max owns a shop."

My eyes draw to his to find them boring into me. "Oh

83

really?" I pose the question to him but the annoying voice of his mother carries across the table.

"He works hard and takes care of things around here. He has a wonderful girlfriend who I hope will be giving me grandchildren soon."

Her words are like ice water being doused over my head. It shouldn't matter, I have Garret, but it's as if any color in the room has been switched off and grey is the only thing that exists. Everything inside me crashes down and reminds me how alone I am.

The food turns sour on my tongue and Max's gaze burns, but not in the pleasant way it did before.

Irrational, Evi.

"Well, that's wonderful for you, Max. Thanks again for feeding me but I really should be going."

"So soon?" she chirps, and I imagine the drink she sips on is acid and it melts her throat. She's trying to scream but her voice box is being eaten and corroded as she does.

"I'll walk you," Max tells me, getting to his feet. I want to tell him to not be stupid. It's next door not the next town over, but the hateful, bitter lady at the table doesn't want me to spend alone time with her precious son and that keeps my lips firmly shut.

The day has turned colder and there are grey clouds looming, threatening us with rain.

"Evi!" Max calls my name to slow me down. I hadn't realized I'd practically run back to the house I now own.

"My mother can be hard work. I thought once my father was out of the way she would find herself again, but instead she became dependent on me."

"Where is your father?"

His jaw tightens. I want to tell him it's okay but I don't.

"We moved here because he was offered work doing construction on the new mall they were going to build here, but investments fell through and the work dried up so fast it sent most people into a tailspin."

The curtain behind him twitches and I know his horrid mother is spying; why do people always like to spy on me?

I stand closer to him, reaching up and wrapping my arms around his shoulders. "He left you."

His strong arms wrap around my waist, pinning my body to his, and my approval lifts the corners of my mouth. He smells so good. "It was a good thing. He was violent towards my mom, and he was a drinker. She gave up her career as a nurse for him and he still hated her."

"I'm sorry," I whisper. And I mean it for him, not for her. Who wouldn't hate her?

It must have been hard on him becoming the man of the house.

"You shouldn't stay in that house alone." His gruff voice tickles over my ear and I pull away and fold my arms over my chest.

"I'll be fine. Haven't you got a girlfriend to get back to?" I punch at his arm in a playful manner, but it's awkward and I regret it straight away.

He takes a quick glimpse over his shoulder at his

mother's house and then whispers, "There's no girlfriend. She moved out of state six months ago, I just don't have the heart to tell mom."

"That's a little pathetic." I'm amused and relieved, although I have no right to be.

He flinches, a small blush creeping up his neck, his large hand rubbing over the back of his collar with his eyes cast down to his feet.

"She wasn't even my girlfriend. She worked for me but my mother is…"

"Pushy?" I finish for him.

"Intrusive. Yes, very pushy. She only has me and she had me late in life so she's paranoid that she won't make it to see grandchildren." His strong, square jaw flexes as he swallows, gaining my attention. "Come back to my place. Shower, sleep. I'll bring you back here tomorrow and help you get the power fixed and get it in a condition fit for purpose if that's what you want to do."

Why is he so worried about me? How close were we as kids?

Alone at night with him in his place.

Thud…

Thud…

Thud…

I could use a hot shower and somewhere to charge my cell phone.

"Okay." I nod in agreement and have to steady myself when his eyes dance, and flecks of gold twinkle from the darker shades.

"Okay, good. Let's get your stuff."

Going inside, I point to my suitcase and he makes a tutting sound and shakes his head. "Just take what you'll need for tonight."

My mouth pops open and I place my hand on my hips. "I don't want to leave anything here in case someone breaks in."

"Who's going to break in here?" he asks, like I'm being utterly ludicrous.

"I don't know. Maybe vandals or trespassers looking to give themselves a fright. Why would your mother be so on guard when I arrived if it wasn't a possibility?"

Pursing his lips, he folds his arms over his chest and they bulge and strain as he does. My eyes focus on the veins popping over his forearms and my stomach bottoms out. I want his hands on me, those fingers inside me. Those puckered lips that are curling at the edges right now to be kissing every inch of my body.

Dirty Evi.

"Evi, what are you thinking about?" he asks, his eyes hooding.

"I'm thinking, *why does he want me to not bring clothes with me.*"

"I didn't say don't bring clothes. Just bring enough for a night."

"Why?" My voice is so breathy I know I'm giving away that I'm wanton. *A needy, dirty girl.*

Pushing his hand through his wild, untamed mane, I think about tugging on the strands while he drives into me. Rough, hard. Punishing me.

He's moving towards me and I'm going to freaking

faint. I've never felt anything so powerful before. Not with Garret, not with Edward. No one.

Palms cup my cheeks, holding my face up to his. "You can't keep looking at me like this. I can practically smell your fucking need and it's going to drive me insane. Look at you. Damn, Evi. You were always beautiful, even as a child, but God, the woman you've evolved into… you're remarkable."

"I'm damaged," I whisper without thought.

Smiling down at me, he speaks with affection, making love to each word. "Frayed at the edges maybe. The colors distorted. But still a masterpiece."

His words are raw and I'm going to combust.

He spins me suddenly, facing me to look out of the front window. I wobble on unsteady feet. I'm dizzy and confused until his arm points over my shoulder towards the front of his mother's house. A black motorbike is parked there. "That's why you can only bring a few things," he whispers into my ear.

Well, shit.

"I can't ride on that with you." I balk.

"You'll be fine."

Spinning back to face him, I shake my head vehemently. "No, Max. I'll fall off that thing."

Biting down on his lip to stop himself laughing, he taps his hand down on the suitcase. "Just pack light."

CHAPTER TEN

EVIL ONE

The rain has already begun falling down, bouncing up from the ground as it makes contact. Everything becomes soaked in seconds, including the bike he wants me to climb onto. He's stuffed my head inside a helmet that smells sweaty and makes me feel like an astronaut. It's heavy and puts pressure on my neck, but I know I have to wear it if I don't want to become sliced salami if, God forbid, we fall off the bike.

"Are you sure we shouldn't wait for the rain to stop?" I ask, thinking the roads will be slippery as all hell right now.

"Just sling your leg over and let's go," he barks, his voice muffled from his own helmet.

He got mine from his mom's house, and from the smell, I'd say it's old and had been left to ferment in there.

He made me slip into an old pair of his sweatpants that, even though they're from when he was much younger, are still too big and have been rolled up at the ankle and down at the waist.

Warning me that the engine gets really hot, and if I place my leg in the wrong place it will scald me, I regret agreeing to this.

I pop open the visor, my breath pushing steam through the air with every exhale. "The seat's wet," I groan, stalling.

Snapping my visor closed, he drags my arm around his back and my leg follows. I climb over the seat until I'm snug against the back of his body. My arms wrap instinctively around his waist, grabbing at the buckle on his pants and clinging on for dear life. I think I hear him groan something but it's too muffled to understand and I panic, wondering if what he's saying is important, a command to keep me safe.

The engine roars to life and vibrates beneath my spread legs. Max's body flexes and ripples with his movements, and before I can prepare my heart, we're taking off. The wind and rain whips around me as Max's body mass completely protects mine, taking all the abuse.

It's a heady sensation, the speed and weightlessness as we speed through the air like a bird. Excitement mixed with fear is a high I always long to reach for and prolong as much as possible. This is the first time I've ever ridden on a bike and I like it. No, scrap that; I love it.

Garret would freak out if he knew I was on the back of a motorcycle. He calls them death traps.

My hands tighten and flex on the buckle and I push myself further into his body, letting his body heat soak into mine. Being like this with him is *freeing*.

We ride for only around fifteen minutes and then the bike is slowing as storefronts come into view. Turning into a parking spot, the bike idles in its place and Max steadies it by placing both of his feet on the ground.

"Climb off!" he shouts, but I'm not ready to let go of him or the high just yet.

His body begins shaking with laughter against my own. "Evi, you're okay. You can get down now." He's mistaking my reluctance for fear.

Climbing from the bike, I lift the helmet and gasp in some fresh air. The rain has dwindled to a light shower, and I'm already wet through so it doesn't bother me. If anything, it reminds me of home. *Swimming*.

Turning the bike off, Max lifts himself from the seat and pulls his own helmet off, placing it on the back of the bike.

"We should stop off and get some wine or beer or… what do you drink?" he asks me, stunning me silent. I can't answer him.

Dazed for a few seconds, I try searching for the answer but I don't know it. What do I like to drink?

"Evi, it's a simple question, not a math equation." He chuckles but he doesn't understand how terrifying the shudder through my body is at not having the answer, as simple as it should be.

Am I forgetting things?

Bringing Garret to the forefront of my mind, I scan through my nights with him. Did we drink wine?

"Evi, are you okay? It's fine if you don't drink. You're barely legal."

"Wine is fine, thank you," I say, turning away from him to hide my flaming cheeks.

Grinning, he nods and takes off walking. Storefronts offer quaint items like dream catchers, and three for two on sticky tape. There's no one around, the street almost empty apart from us. A bar on the corner has a few stragglers talking and smoking outside and there's a faint humming of music oozing from the crack in the door.

We walk a few blocks and cross the road towards a convenience store.

The bell overhead chimes as Max pushes through; an older man looks up from the paper he's reading behind the counter. Max nods to him and he waves a hand briefly in response until he see me come into view behind Max. The paper now forgotten, he stands. "Who is your lovely friend, Maxwell?"

The groan from Max's lips is soft and only audible to me because I'm so close to him.

"A friend, Tim."

Max opens a fridge and pulls a six pack out and then reaches behind him and takes my hand, generating all the blood in my body to pool in my lower stomach. Pulling me down an aisle stocked with bottle after bottle of alcohol, Max looks to me expectantly. He wants me to choose what I like. Crap.

"White or red?"

The air con above us clatters and chokes as hot air pumps from it, making a bead of sweat blister on my hairline.

"Red," I tell him, because I prefer the color red to white.

Like many times today, his eyes hold mine, searching, probing, wanting.

Turning his attention to the bottles on the shelves, he picks up a couple of different bottles before returning them to their place. I reach out and wrap my hands around one of the bottlenecks and tap the label.

"This one." His eyes pop wide and we both chuckle at the name.

'Flirt' is emblazoned in red across the label.

The bell overhead chimes again and Max is tall enough to see over the shelves. The amusement from before escapes his features and a stoic expression takes its place.

"Come on." He takes the bottle from me and places it in the crook of his arm. He frog marches me to the counter and pulls out a few twenties, dropping them onto Tim's newspaper.

"Death toll up to three hundred, all these weeks later." Tim tuts, pointing to an article about a train accident.

"Hmm" Max grunts spinning us towards the exit, the shopper who entered just after us initiating the shift in his demeanor is now blocking the exit.

She's an older woman; not old like his mom, maybe in her early forties. Her hair is pinned up on top of her head and she has a sprinkling of small brown freckles scattering across a perfectly trim nose. Blue eyes search his, her complexion fair with a rosy glow. Her slim shoulders are stiff, leading down to a svelte body. She's wearing a raincoat tied at the waist.

Looking between the two of us, her lips move but no sound comes out.

There's recognition in the way she looks at me, and the more I stare at her, the more familiar she becomes to me.

"You're a good girl, Evi, and should celebrate your birthday. Let me speak to your mom and dad."

A gasp echoes from my lips and I step back like I've been struck by lightning.

Her scent fills my nose but it's a memory of the past, not because she's come closer. A sweet, sickly scent wraps around me.

I see her in my mind's eye, writing on a chalkboard in front of a class. My class.

"Miss Groom?" The words are falling from my lips without permission, and the way her mouth drops open and tears spring to her eyes in response, I wish I could stuff them back inside. Dread, the same one that keeps coming over me in warning, tingles in my spine.

"Evi?"

"Come on, Evi," Max demands, taking my hand and dragging me past her.

She moves fast, grabbing onto my arm. "Wait!" she cries, and my body reacts on instinct.

Slapping her hand away, I wrench my hand free from Max's hold and shove her backwards. "Don't touch me!" I'm unclear where the hostility comes from but it's deep-rooted and fiery. I like the way it makes me feel. The rage is like an old friend visiting, one you've missed and embrace with open arms.

"I'm sorry," she chokes, but Max reaffirms his grip on me, tugging me away.

We're walking but my head is cloudy and I don't even notice how far we've come or that we're inside now.

"Make yourself at home." He grunts and the room swims around me.

"Max, who was that woman?" My heart is beating hard in my chest and I feel out of breath.

"You said her name. You must know," he retorts, chucking his house keys down on a metal dining table situated in an open plan apartment. The walls are brick and the floors dark hardwood. Huge windows stretching from ceiling to floor allow the light to bleed through, igniting the space in a glorious glow.

A worn leather couch and old wooden coffee table along with the metal dining table and benches on either side are the only furniture in the entire place. There's an old motorbike positioned on one of the walls like art.

The kitchen borders the living space, running the entire width of the apartment. A black iron staircase twirls in the center of the room, leading to an open plan bedroom above.

"What's clicking around that head of yours?" he asks, moving into my space. Is he emitting some form of pheromone? "Did you remember something?" Concern dips his brows.

"Just her name. A school. She's a teacher, right?"

His head bounces up and down, confirming. Taking

my hands in his, he leads me to the couch and gently guides me to sit down. "She was your teacher. You were close with her."

"Really?"

"We were with her that night."

We?

"What night?"

Shifting in his seat, his jaw locks. Squeezing his hand, I plead with my eyes for him not to stop talking.

"The night everything happened. It was your birthday."

The badge.

The 'nine' badge on the hospital table when I woke up flashes in my mind. I kept that thing; it's the only item I have from my previous life.

"Why was I with my teacher?"

The room morphs, the air thickening and closing in around me.

"Because she felt sorry for you. She wanted you to have a day just for you."

Thud...

"Why?"

"Because you were a child whose family abused you," he snaps, getting to his feet and pushing his hands through his hair.

Family.

Family abused you.

Not singular.

Tears spring to my eyes and burn the tear ducts. "Was it my brothers? Is that why you hated them?"

He's pacing the apartment now but I can't move. I feel

like I'm drowning in ice, the shards freezing over my heart.

"Your father had some weird, fucked up belief that you were theirs. Useable to your brothers."

Anger and disgust screw up his features and cause a manifestation so fierce it reminds me of a shadow growing in firelight, expanding, swallowing everything once created by light.

"So, she felt sorry for me?"

His movements stop and he looks over at me, steam almost visible from his ears.

"Did you hear what I said?"

My brother—brothers—abused me

"Yes!" I snap, getting to my feet. "You think I don't know I was abused, Max? Is that what you think you're protecting me from?"

Pushing his sweatpants down my legs, taking my panties with them, I place one foot on the couch and leave the other on the floor so I'm open for him. I reach for the hem of my shirt and pull it over my head so I'm completely naked.

He's solidified to the spot, his eyes bulging and heat tinging his cheeks.

"What are you doing?" He pants, his body deflating like I poked a pin in him and let all the tension and hot air out.

"Showing you. The scars already told me the secrets you think you're keeping from me!"

His feet move toward me, water glistening in his eyes. Dropping to his knees in front of me, he takes my foot from the couch and pushes it back into the sweatpants leg, repeating the process with the other foot. He slips the material up my legs and over my hips until they're covering me. He doesn't get to his feet. Instead, his arms wrap around my waist and pin my body to him. His shoulders shake as he burrows his head against my stomach, and the need to run my fingers through his hair is overwhelming.

The warmth of his body pressed against mine ebbs the chills I'd been feeling moments before.

"They deserved to die, Evi. Your mother knew it too."

"Did I deserve to die?" I whisper, so quietly I'm not sure he hears me.

"No, and you didn't."

When he gets to his feet, his eyes flick to my still exposed breasts and I bend to fetch my top, turning to slip it over my head. His gasp causes my head to snap back around.

His fingertips stroke down over my back, dancing over the scars there. "I remember the day you got these."

I'm slowly turning to face him when something comes over him, a tornado snapping and swirling his features. Shaking his head, he hurries away in the other direction.

I hear a door slam and search the walls for where he could have gone. A room in the far corner is the only place that's not on display.

A bathroom, I surmise.

I go to the bag I brought with me and retrieve my cell phone and charger, searching the room for an outlet to plug it into. There's a spare socket in the kitchen by the boiling pot.

My cell doesn't light up straight away when I plug it in.

Instead, a red exclamation mark lights the screen.

Max returns, holding a folded towel in his arms, offering it to me.

"Did you want to take a shower? I'll heat some food and pour you some wine."

It feels natural being around him, like we've always known each other. It's easy and soothing. Garret would have so much to say about that, and if he had come with me, I wouldn't be here right now with Max.

For the first time ever, I'm grateful he didn't take me up on the invitation.

"Sure, that sounds good. Thank you."

Taking the towel from him, I make my way to the room he just left, and true to my theory, it is a bathroom, only there's no bath, just a tiled room with a dipped floor with a drain in the middle and a shower head hanging from the ceiling. The buttons on the wall control the temperature and speed. There's a toilet cornered off by a glass wall in the corner.

I slip from my clothes and place them on the lid of the toilet seat.

Turning the temperature up high, I let the water cascade over me, soaking me. I spend so much time in water, it's a wonder I don't grow gills.

All the information thrown at me today rattles around inside my mind, trying to form pictures that make sense. When I think about who these people must have been, it leaves a hollow hole in my chest, wider and deeper than not knowing. I've found solace only in the discovery of Max. He was a good thing in my life before; I can feel it deep in my soul. A friend who searched for me. Maybe he's the reason I've never felt like I could let my past go. Deep down, was I searching for him too? Just being around him makes me almost content; it's such a bizarre reaction to have in such a small timeframe.

Can a flower blossom in dry earth where nothing grows?

Wrapping my body in the towel, I realize I left my bag with my clean clothes on the table. My hair hangs in a curly mass down my back and I tighten the knot I've created in the towel to keep it from falling down.

Max has his back to me when I open the door and step out of the bathroom. The space seems larger than before. Maybe it's me who's shrinking.

I may just fade away to dust.

He's moving around from the stove to the counter, chopping and throwing things into a pan in the kitchen. There's a soft melody humming from a radio on the window ledge. He tosses what smells like an omelet in a frying pan.

Taking my bag in hand, I rummage through it for the shorts and tee I brought with me to sleep in. I slip them up my legs under the towel, and when I'm done, I fold the towel and startle when I notice he's stopped moving and is staring at me.

"I made eggs," he says, holding the pan in his hand.

"Great. Thank you."

I sit at the table and finger brush my hair, annoyed at myself for not bringing a brush with me.

Max places a plate in front of me and serves up the

omelet dish he's created. He places a glass next to the plate and begins to pour the red wine into it, stopping only a quarter of the way full.

Taking the seat opposite me, I notice he's not having any food.

"Not hungry?" I ask, slightly uncomfortable to eat without him.

"I forgot to pick up more eggs at the store." He flinches, embarrassment tickling his features.

Visions of him rushing us out of there flicker through my thoughts.

"We can share," I say, getting to my feet and searching his kitchen for cutlery. I locate a fork in the drainer over the sink.

Picking up the plate, I move closer to him and hand him the spare fork. He grins down at me and helps himself to a mouthful. I take a smaller piece into my mouth and flavor bursts over my tongue inciting a groan. "Wow, that's amazing."

His grin broadens, reaching his eyes. "Thanks. It's the only thing I can cook."

"I'm not sure I want to share now," I tease, moving the plate away from him, and a hearty chuckle rumbles from his chest.

"I like your laugh," I tell him.

He doesn't speak, and I know if I look up, he will be staring at me again.

Light rain pitter-patters against the windowpanes like a melody, inciting a bubble of unease to simmer in my veins.

"Tell me how we met," I say, sipping from the glass and

refraining from gagging on the sharp, dry taste coating my throat.

Picking up a bottle of beer, he swigs, and by the time he pulls it away from his lips, it's half gone.

"I'd just moved there and saw you in your garden."

"Hey, I'm Max. What's there to do for fun around here?"

"You didn't answer me. Ignored me like I didn't exist, and then your brother Lucian came outside holding a belt. He handed it to you and said your father was ready to give you your punishment."

I listen intently. The scars on my back hum and phantom whips ignite over my flesh.

A man's voice barks in the back of my subconscious.

"Count, Evi, or I'll start from the beginning."

The sound of the belt like a whip whistling through the air, cracking as it makes contact. A fiery blaze opening up the flesh.

"You just took the belt like it was routine." He guzzles the rest of his drink down until the bottle is empty. He drops it to the table and pushes it away from him.

"That night, my dad was arguing with my mom over some bullshit I can't even remember, but I crept out the back of the house and found the water. You were sitting in it like a bathtub." He curls his lips, but it's sorrow, not happiness that causes it. "Damn, Evi. Your back was all torn up. I went back to my house and got some of my mom's old swabs and things from her kit and cleaned you up. I swore to you that I'd never sit by and let that happen again. That I'd tell someone."

A stray tear leaks from my eyes for the little girl I used

to be.

"And did you?" I ask, taking another sip from my glass. "Tell anyone?"

He nods his head. "Miss Groom."

The teacher from earlier.

"The way she was looking at you, the whole situation was odd. She didn't know I was here at first and things were tense. Is there more there than you let on?" I ask.

Getting to his feet, the chair scrapes against the hard floor and reminds me of nails down a chalkboard. He opens the fridge and returns with another bottle of beer. Popping the lid off, he fiddles with it, passing it through his fingers and back again.

"It's complicated."

It always is.

"Elaborate."

"After what happened with you, she stopped teaching and fell into a depression. She went off the grid for years. I hadn't even thought about her and then one night when I was out celebrating my birthday in an awful bar in the next town over, she was there, waitressing."

Tapping my fingers on the stem of my glass, I gulp down the repulsion I'm already feeling at what he's going to say next.

"She broke down crying and slobbering all over me. She spoke about you and it brought up so much emotion that I hadn't dealt with myself. I brought her back here to talk more. I was pretty lit. One thing led to another."

Whore. Where? On this table? That couch? In your bed?

"That's kind of gross," I say, thinking of the age gap and her being our teacher once. I don't consider my behavior with Edward gross, but this isn't about me.

He chuckles but it dies in his chest. "It's weird. I can't explain it but it made me feel close to you somehow. Like if she hadn't forgotten you and I hadn't, you were there in some way. Alive. Real. Home." Scrunching up his nose, he tilts the bottle back and drains it in one.

My cell phone suddenly shrills into the room with incoming text messages, and I almost knock over my glass from the shock of it.

"You're popular." He grins, getting up and retrieving my cell from the kitchen.

He's looking down at the screen. Intrusive, but I would probably have done the same thing. "This Garret guy wants you to call him."

Handing me the phone, he retakes his seat and stares at the cell like it's a bomb in my hand. I have a lot of missed calls and texts from Garret, telling me to call him.

"So who is he?" Max asks, a slight defensive edge in his tone.

That's such a complicated question to answer.

"He's my boyfriend," I say, and the room cools and the rain appears to get louder as my breathing slows and my pulse thunders in my ears.

The silence is deafening and I want to take it back, but it's the truth, and I owe him that because it's what I'm asking for in return. The wine begins to circulate through my bloodstream, making my mind hazy, and the room expands. A yawn pushes past my lips and the eggs sit cold in front of me.

"You want to get some sleep?" Max asks, breaking the uncomfortable silence.

"Yeah. I could sleep."

He points to the room above us. "You can take the bed. I'll take the couch."

"No. I don't mind taking the couch, honestly. I don't want to takeover your place."

"Evi, take the bed."

Making my way up the iron staircase, I sense him watching me and heat fizzles throughout my body, sending a tingling sensation up my spine.

His room consists of a bed and nothing else. Crawling over it, I collapse against the pillow and groan when his earthy scent cocoons me. Gathering the duvet up into a plump rectangle, I wrap one leg and one arm over it and pretend it's Max laying with me.

I should text Garret back to put his mind at rest, but in this moment, I don't want to.

CHAPTER ELEVEN

KING OF HELL

The rain is pounding against my flesh like crystal glass, each droplet sharp and bitter against my skin.

Shivers wrack my body and blood coats my hands.

The night sky is so black; no stars shine. A knife juts from my stomach and I'm crying, trying to pull it free.

A faceless body stands in front of me, and in the next breath, the knife is in their hand and not my gut.

Panic seizes my chest and my breathing labors.

There's no sound apart from the rain hammering against a tin roof. Someone is calling my name and a child is crying.

I look through the back gate of my house into the trees where the sound carries.

Eleanor.

The name whispers from my lips and a gaping hole punches through my chest.

"Evi. Drop the knife."

I battle with the crying and the voice in front of me. I want to follow the misery of the child but my feet are rooted to the spot and I'm so cold; my body feels numb.

"Evi," the voice says again, and it's clearer this time. Not that of a stranger, but familiar.

The sky lightens and stars pop like fireworks. My conscious thoughts battle the ones in my dreams.

"Goddammit, Evi!" The words punch the air and my eyes flitter open and shut.

I gasp for air and my hands fly to my chest to massage the ache there. Rain pours down on me, running through my eyelashes and distorting the presence in front of me.

A glint of a blade catches my eye and a scream rips from my chest.

"No, please!" I cry out, stepping back and almost tumbling over an old plant pot.

"Evi, you're okay."

Max's voice penetrates the haze I'm in and the shuddering of my body takes over.

Images of me being in this place only smaller attack me in a barrage of mixed jigsaw pieces.

"Why are you holding a knife?" I whimper.

Max looks down at the blade in his hand and drops it to the floor.

"You had it. I just took it from you."

What?

It's then it dawns on me where I am. I'm back at the house, standing in the pouring rain in my nightclothes, and Max is topless, looking down at me, terrified.

The soles of my feet sting and I hiss and lift my right foot to see the old wound from the lake house has opened up and is bleeding, running away with the rain water.

"What the hell are you doing here, Evi? I woke up to my mother calling, saying you were in here holding a knife."

I look up at his mother's house to see the lights on and her nosy face peering out at us.

"I… I sleep walk," I murmur, embarrassment and fear seating themselves in my chest.

"It's an hour walk from my apartment to here," he says, astonishment in his voice.

"I heard crying. A child."

He stiffens and his mouth snaps shut, doing that jaw ticking he does.

"It felt so vivid."

"You were dreaming. You should have told me you sleep walk. I would have stayed awake and watched over you."

"Why?"

"Why what?"

"Why would you have stayed awake to watch over me, Max?"

"So you didn't walk four fucking miles in the pitch black with no shoes or coat on."

"But why do you even care?"

I'm desperate to know why he's being so nice to me. Why he cares so much, and why I feel so connected to him. His eyes flicker and flit as if searching for the right answer.

"I've always cared. You might not remember me, Evi. You might not remember us, but I do. Every single detail. And there hasn't been a day, Jesus, a fucking minute when I haven't thought about you."

He cares. He really cares about me. This isn't like Edward or even Garret, who couldn't be bothered to come here, or to the lake house.

"I'm cold and your mother is staring at me." I change the subject and he sniffs and pushes back the wet strands of hair that have fallen in his face.

He takes a quick glance up at his mother's window and waves a hand. Looking back at me, he offers his hand. "Come on. Let's go back to my place and get you dry."

I take the hand he's offering and follow him through the gate into his mother's garden and through her house. "Go to sleep, Mom. I'll be over tomorrow." Her dagger eyes scald into my back as we leave.

"She's trouble, Maxwell," she croaks, and I can't argue with that, because maybe I am.

He leads me down the garden path and I sigh when I see a truck and not his bike. He helps me inside and goes around to the driver's side. His words play on repeat in my head.

"There hasn't been a day, Jesus, a fucking minute when I haven't thought about you."

When his door slams shut, I launch myself over the

seats into his lap. It's awkward. My knee hits the door and my foot lodges inside the cup holder, but none of that matters

He startles and turns rigid under me at first, but within seconds, his body softens and his arms clutch me to him. We're both dripping with rain water and the condensation steams the windows and my flesh. We stare at each other, saying a thousand words without sound.

It's unexplainable how my soul recognizes his so passionately, but it does.

His breath, hot and needy, disperses over my sensitive skin with every exhale, his jaw locked and eyes heavy with lust.

"I want you so bad," I confess, and like striking a match, we ignite.

Our lips collide, battling for control, his hot, probing tongue dominating and exploring every inch of my mouth. Grinding my body against his to cause some friction against my clit to relieve the pressure building there, I thrash and rock against him. He moans in response, thickening beneath me. He's so much bigger than me that he maneuvers me around like I'm a doll and he's my master.

The space is small, but so am I.

Heavy hands pull and tear at my clothing, ripping my top and exposing the wet, sticky skin beneath. His hot lips brush over my skin, finding my hard, begging nipple and sucking it into his mouth.

I want to move more but the confines of the truck keep me restricted, like invisible thread tying me down.

My pussy throbs, crying out for relief. Taking his hand

in mine, I push it between my legs and buck over it.

His fingers reach the waistband of my shorts and slip beneath it, finding my hot, wet juices already flowing between my folds.

"Jesus," he breathes against my body, his hot breath setting me on fire.

His fingers explore and nudge until they slip effortlessly inside me. They're long and thick, and I buckle under the intrusion, moaning out and throwing my head back.

Moving them in and out of me with rapid succession, he teases my clit with the pad of his thumb.

My body bounces to keep pace. He's fucking me with just his fingers and it's still the best I've ever had.

My lips part and I gaze into his lust-filled stare, our lips brushing against each other's as we dance in pleasure.

Reaching down, I fight with his zipper to free the hard granite I can feel confined inside. His fingers slow their pace inside me and I groan in protest.

"I think … we shouldn't…"

"Shh." I place my lips to his, kissing and biting

"Don't think, just feel." I push my bare chest against his and rejoice in the sensation of being skin to skin with him.

Freeing his cock from the hold of his jeans, he gasps when I brush down the length with the palm of my hand.

Nostril flaring, his body is rigid beneath me, and I know the fight he's battling over the right thing to do.

I hate doing the right thing.

Taking his cock in my tiny fist, I use my other hand to pull my short leg to the side.

His hand moves from inside me and I replace it with

the tip of his cock. Lined up at my entrance, he breathes my name and I lower myself down over him, relishing the stretch as I completely sheath him.

His cock is thick and long, much like his body, and it hurts to sit on him in the most delicious of ways.

A sharp pain twinges in my stomach with every full bounce I take, gyrating my hips. Smoothing over my tits with his palms, his fingers find my nipples, rolling them and pinching.

"Are you sure you want this?"

It's a stupid question because I'm already full to the brim with him.

I don't answer with words, instead I contract my pussy walls around him and savor his hiss.

The windows have steamed up but I wonder if his mother is watching, and hopefully having a heart attack at the show.

His palms move down to my ass cheeks, squeezing and guiding me up and over him, skin slapping skin and the wet juices slurping as he plunges so deep inside me he may never be able to leave.

His lips find mine again, soft and then urgent as he embraces me, pulling me tight against him.

Our mouths hang open against each other's, bursts of kissing and then panting emanating from our spent bodies.

Running my hands through the soft wet strands of his hair as my entire body tenses and spasms, my thighs clamp against him and my hips thrust up; one, two, and then my stomach muscles pull so taut I may be stuck like that forever.

Hot, white, blinding pleasure licks through me, sending my body into convulsions.

A cry rips from my lips as I scrunch my eyes closed, the pleasure so intense I think I actually leave my body and float above myself.

Max forces his hips upwards, prolonging my release, and with it his own ripples over him, throbbing and contracting until hot ribbons pulse inside me, making me aware that Max has followed me over the edge. His tongue flutters like a bird's wing against my lips.

Sighing, his lips flurry over my reddened cheeks, and he whispers, "You feel so damn good."

Nibbling on his ear, I inhale and exhale and a giggle leaves me.

Our sweat sticks us together like glue and I don't think I could ever be close enough to him. I want to become water, seep into his skin and live just under the surface, feeling his blood rush through his veins every day for the rest of my life.

The high of sex makes me weightless and careless in its euphoria, but it's short-lived.

The small space begins to suffocate me as the fluids from our bodies begin to seep out of me, staining my upper thighs, the sweat turning cold and dry on my skin.

Lifting from Max's now flaccid cock, indignity begins to taunt me, sending a sprinkle of goose bumps over my flesh and heat to my cheeks.

Dirty Evi.

Why does this happen to me? I don't regret being with him. I enjoyed how he made me feel, so why does the need to cleanse myself wash over me?

My hand darts for the door handle and I spill out of the truck onto the damp concrete.

Max quickly tucks himself back into his pants and leans down over me to pick me back up, but my heart seizes and the eyes peering down at me don't match the older, rugged face but instead morph into a boy. Pain explodes in my stomach and my hand pushes against the scar.

Rain pelts down over me and Max has moved, trying to step over me, but I scramble to get up, the asphalt cutting into my skin as I do.

"Evi." He says my name so gently that a tear leaks from my eyes.

Holding his hands up in surrender, he looks broken, like me. So damaged that we will probably never be whole.

"You're freezing."

My body shudders in response. I want him to invade my space, wrap me in his arms, and squeeze until the air constricts and I asphyxiate against his flesh.

Dirty Evi.

I already long to feel him again. Pressure builds between my hips and the sore ache turns to hot need just thinking of the pain mixed with pleasure I'd feel if he took me roughly against the truck bed right now.

Dirty Evi.

He steps towards me, still shirtless, and I sprint away from him.

The rain whips and cuts at my flesh. I dart through an alley towards the back of the houses.

The dark night sky is being swallowed by the trees as they shield me beneath them.

My blood burns in my veins, a contrast to the rain assaulting me. Tears mix and bleed with the droplets cascading down my face.

My feet scream in pain as brush and stones are relentless against the soles. Branches lash and tear at my exposed body.

Heavy pounding slapping against the wet floor sounds behind me and I know Max is following, and I'm relieved.

I need him to snap me from whatever is driving me. Drag me away, save me from myself.

My dreams come crashing down around me and I'm so muddled up inside my thoughts, I don't know what's real and what's the dream world anymore.

Sounds of animals and wind rustling through the trees howl and scream in my ears, but I push on.

My lungs burn and my ribs protest. My legs weaken and I hit the water, wading in up to my waist.

The cold force stills my breath, despite already being soaked and freezing.

The dirty lake offers comfort.

The rain almost feels hot in comparison to the cold, compressing weight of the water flowing over me.

Heavy breathing and the sound of boots crunching over stones and rubble signal Max's presence.

The moon casts a blue glow over the water that ripples from my intrusion.

Sobs ricochet through me and I don't know why I'm crying.

"Evi," Max whispers. Broken words tremble from his lips.

"Come out of there."

I turn to face him.

Worry and concern cause the corners of his lips to pull down. He looks paler under the hue of moonlight.

"Do you want to save me, Max?" I ask, admitting for the first time to myself that I actually may need it.

He drops to his knees, holding his hands out towards me.

"You don't need saving, Evi. You needed to be found. Appreciated. Worshipped."

"Why? Because I'm beautiful? A good fuck?" I shout, spiteful and venomous.

His head drops for a second and then lifts, his eyes trying to convey all the emotion inside him.

"You are beautiful, Evi. But love doesn't see with its eyes, hear with sound, feel with touch; it connects with its mind, and once it does, there's no going back."

My arms wrap around my waist to offer myself security.

I want to start my life over again, change everything that I am.

Except him.

"I just want to feel clean. Clear. I want to understand these needs inside me. Why do I come to the water?"

Getting to his feet, he wades into the water until he's mere feet from me.

"You used to come here when someone did things they shouldn't have to you."

A faint breeze carries across the water, blowing my hair, and with it a sound of a child crying.

My head whips to the side, searching the tree line. Nothing.

"I need to clean away their touches."

His hand reaches for mine. Warm and strong.

"Have you ever been followed, or thought you were being followed? Maybe had a dream so vivid that you had done something wrong, really wrong, and the police were coming for you?"

"Sure," he answers, his features pinching in confusion.

"And just as their blue lights flash over your body, they suddenly race past. They weren't coming for you after all, but your heart is skipping so fast. You're on the brink of toppling over the edge of a cliff, and at the last second, the wind blows you back from it. Sticky skin, an empty pit in your gut?"

He nods. "Once or twice. Why?"

Pain contorts my face.

"I feel that way all the time. The trees around me sway in mourning. The creatures have broken wings and the water holds ghosts. My past has me by the throat. I'm in a choke hold, gasping, begging for air."

He closes the space with another step towards me.

"I want to pull a little of peace of heaven down just for you so you feel the beauty in the world," he whispers.

The chaos inside me retreats and I'm just a girl standing with a boy who, moments earlier, had my pleasure swarming through me like a thousand bees around a honey tree, the buzzing and fluttering chaotic and wild but poetic and blissful.

"Why bring me heaven when we've already raised hell and I liked the way it burned?" I tease, letting him take me in his arms.

I climb him, wrapping my arms around his neck and dipping my head into the crook of his neck and my legs around his waist.

"I'm sorry I ran."

Clinging to me, he walks from the water and takes me over to some rocks where he said the boy was murdered.

Much like with the death of Daniel, it doesn't evoke any emotion inside me.

Knowing someone was murdered right here doesn't make me want to move. I simply don't care.

Dropping to his haunches, Max examines the cuts on my feet. "They're a mess, Evi. We should go back to mom's and let her fix you up."

I'd rather bleed out than let that woman touch me.

"Do you think there's something broken inside me? The veins knotted? The bones bent?"

"Evi. There's nothing broken within you. You suffered trauma and your mind had its own way of dealing with it."

An orange tinge kisses the skyline and I realize it's the sun and morning is breaking through the night. It highlights Max at my feet.

"You look like an angel down there," I jest, biting my lip. His muscles pull and tighten over his back.

His broad shoulders flex and swell as he dabs over a cut on my sole. Beads of water shine and drip over him.

His eyes creep up at me through his thick lashes to

hold me in their gaze. "I have demons, Evi, but you bring them to their knees."

"Why?" I honestly need to know.

"To worship their queen."

Thud...

"Are you saying I'm a demon too? I'm my namesake?"

He smiles so softly my heart skips. "Remember, the devil wasn't always shrouded in darkness, Evi. He was once an angel."

He rises up to his full height and my body dims in his shadow. Nerve endings pop and zap.

All I want to feel is him wrapped around me.

I know I'm not normal. The way I crave sexual attention isn't right. My father was the devil.

He created his own hell in our house and now I only feel at home when I'm embracing that darkness.

"I'm going to have to carry you back." His eyes drop to my panting chest lifting my bare breasts up and down in offering.

Grasping onto him, I spread my legs and pull him to stand between them, reveling in the heat of his body against mine.

Lifting his hand in mine, I spread his fingers wide and place his hand at my throat.

I want him to squeeze and punish me. Thrust into me and cause the skin to break as the rock tears into me.

I find beauty in pain and darkness because of the horrors that bestowed me in light.

"What are you doing?"

I'm playing games that I shouldn't be. Pushing limits

with him.

"Hurt me. Fuck me," I beg. "Steal my breath, Max."

His hand wraps around my throat with such ease it's as if it was made to fit there.

His anger is a manifestation of heartache. Sorrow. Guilt? But as his hand tightens and I beam up at him, one emotion stands above all the rest.

Fear.

Fear for me, for what I need, but most of all fear because he likes it too.

The power, the control, the pain, the burn.

The darkness.

"Fuck me, Max. Fuck me!" I shout.

His hand tightens around my throat and my words become mute.

He pulls me towards his lips and we collide, urgent and ruthless, sucking, nipping, tasting.

The craving is so intense I feel it like a drug being injected straight to the vein.

"What do you want, Evi?" He exhales, breathless, the hard planes of his body like granite against the soft, supple curves of my own.

"I want to sink so deep within each other that we don't know where one begins and the other finishes."

I lick over his chest, biting at his chin.

"Let's explore all the dark corners together. Follow the pull of lust and exploit our desires."

My hands drop to unbutton his jeans and free his cock from its confines.

"Let's make new memories, new secrets to keep from

the world."

My palm dances up and down his shaft as he sucks and teases my neck.

"Fuck me hard. Pull my hair and treat me how you feel, Max. How hard do you want to take me?"

"Hard." He growls.

"You disappeared on me, just left me after everything we went through."

Anger and old wounds open from within him, speaking truth he wouldn't have spoken before.

"Punish me."

Abandoning my neck, he moves from my body, the cold chill washing over me in a rush.

"Is that what you really want?" he snarls, the demons coming out to play.

"Yes!" I scream at him, slapping his chest.

Yanking me from the rock, he spins me around and bends me face down over it, jerking my wet shorts down my legs and tossing them behind him.

The expanse of his palm spreads over my spine, pinning me down.

"Is this what you want me to do" he roars, kicking my legs apart.

The rough surface of the stone irritates and burns the soft peaks of my nipples.

Heat from his body covers my backside and then all the air whizzes out of my lungs when he rams inside me, seating himself to the hilt.

Explosions of pain, scorching and intense, burst inside my walls.

Yes.

Yes.

Wrapping a fist in my hair, he heaves my head back and juts his hips forward, generating a scream to rip out of me.

Pleasure, pain, the beautiful edge between the two hold me suspended in its frayed strings.

"You want me to punish and fuck you?"

"Yes."

"Ruin and destroy you."

"Yes."

"Abuse and mistreat you."

"Yes."

"Like they did?"

No.

"Like your father?"

No.

"Your brothers?"

No.

No.

"Yes."

Sobbing, my chest constricts so tight I can't gain air.

I'm disgusting.

His firmness leaves my body and I sag over the rock, heaving and crying, trying to grasp onto my sanity.

"I won't be like them for you. I can't," he mumbles, and his footfalls fade away from me.

I don't know how long I lay here.

The sun creeps over the horizon, sending its warm rays over my skin. My eyes sting and my face feels sore from all the tears I've shed.

My eyes close and open slowly as exhaustion bleeds into my bones.

A boy's face plagues me behind my eyelids.

Blond shaven hair spikes up over a round head. Blue eyes, small and invasive, stare at me. Skinny arms flail next to him as he walks with a swagger. His skinny, waif-like body comes to a stop next to the water where I'm sitting.

My insides hurt and the cool water eases the pain.

"Hey." He speaks and my insides corrode.

"Why have you followed me, Luke?" I grumble, looking around him to see if my brothers are coming here too. My sanctuary. The water is my solitude to wash away the darkness. But he's alone.

"Lucian told me you were out here. He said you've got something for me."

Liar, liar, pants on fire.

Standing up, I grab the towel Max always leaves out on the rocks for me. They always smell of flowers from the soap his mom uses. My mom doesn't use any soap and we all have to share the same towel.

Moving towards the rocks, I brush the furry material over my skin and then tighten it over my body.

"I don't have anything for you."

"You have a kiss." He smirks, coming towards me. His thin lips purse and come at my face.

I back away, shaking my head. "Lucian wouldn't like that, Luke," I say, feeling dirty and angry at him following me out here. And thinking he can touch me like that, kiss me. He can't. I won't allow it. He's no one.

Thin fingers paw at me and try to snatch away the towel. "I know what you do with them, Evi. I'll tell."

Tell who? Who would care?

"Leave me alone!" I shout, backing further into the rocks.

He tries to follow but his foot slips and twists. Screaming out in pain, he falls to the floor. "You bitch. Look what you did."

My eyes drop to his ankle wedged between two small boulders. It's pointing at a weird angle and he's writhing in pain.

"Go get help, you stupid little whore!"

The pain, anger, the broken dirty pieces of my soul fragments. I have a volcano inside waiting to erupt but I'm still so cold. My mind, my soul.

I don't like it, the way they make me feel. The pain they inflict. The worthless acts they make me perform.

It has to start somewhere.

The fight back. It has to start sometime. Before I'm ruined forever.

What better place than right here? My lake. What better time than now? The greedy little pig, stuck like the fool he is.

His arm lashes out to me, gripping the towel around me, yanking it from my body.

Laughter, rapturous and mocking, roars from his chest as I stand there, bare and humiliated.

"You don't even have any pussy hair," he mocks.

Am I supposed to have hair there?

"I'm going stuff my finger in there and make you bleed, you little brat," he barks.

"Go get your brother to help me."

"I'm going to tell him what you said." I test him and his face pales.

"He won't believe you."

Maybe.

"What will you tell him? Why you're back here?" I push.

His face gives him away and confirms what I thought. They don't know he's even here.

"I'll cut your lying tongue out of your head, Evi Devil," he snaps.

My fingers brush over a rock at my foot.

No you won't.

"Evi!" Max bellows.

"He made me do it," I gasp, pointing to the body.

The blood coats my fingers. The warm crimson stain looks familiar on my skin, these hands soaking the liquid up.

"Made you do what?"

"He was trying to touch me. He said bad things."

"Evi."

"I had to do it!"

"There's no one there, Evi."

My eyes try to focus on the boy but he's not there. It's just rocks and **nothing.**

Sucking at the air to fill my lungs, I place my hand to my chest to feel the steady thud. "The boy."

Max's brow dips. "I shouldn't have left you here. I went to get you some bandages and shoes."

He holds up a bag. Scanning the palms of my hands, I see no blood there.

The dream was so real.

"The boy who died here," I breathe.

"Evi, don't," he warns.

"Was his name Luke?"

Dropping the bag to the floor, he places his hands on his hips and looks off over the water.

The sun has risen and has begun drying all the damp from the rain, leaving an earthy scent pungent in the air.

"He doesn't matter."

"I think I may have done something to him."

The confession vibrates in my chest. Did I kill him?

"Evi, that's not true. You're just confused."

Shaking my head vehemently, a tear leaks from my eye. Tolerance of abuse when tested can transform a person from victim to monster.

"I think I liked it. He deserved it," I choke.

Max doesn't screw his face up in disgust at my admission or back away in fear, he just stares at me, devouring me right through to my damaged soul.

"I told you. He was an asshole."

A laugh cackles from me. It's unnatural and I'm not sure it's even humor.

"The monsters ravaged and ruined me so I became one."

"You're not a monster."

"Then what am I if not a monster? What makes a monster not a monster?" I snuffle.

"A monster's not a monster when it's loved, Evi."

*Who loves me? **Him?***

"Are you a monster?" I breathe.

He shakes his head and shrugs.

"Doesn't matter if I am. Not all beasts do atrocious things. Sometimes the evil around us creates a monster because the world sometimes needs one to rid the world of worse monsters."

"Is that what my mom did?"

A blank expression steals the light from his eyes and he reaches down and picks up the bag.

"I need to clean your feet before you end up with an infection."

Okay.

CHAPTER TWELVE

BRUTE

Walking around the house I grew up in makes sickness stir.

Max brought me back here to get clean clothes from my suitcase and offered to take me to his mother's while he cooks us something to eat in there, but I refused.

I didn't like her old, knowing eyes boring into me.

Scooping my hair up into a messy bun, I look around at the dust and debate asking Max to take me to the store for some cleaning products.

I already know I don't want to stay here though, and cleaning up old mess created by people I should never have wanted to remember has lost its appeal.

Walking back to the room where the beds and dried blood was, I force myself to open the door to shock myself into remembering something. Anything.

Thud...

What the hell?

The room is empty. No beds, no carpet, no blood. Stepping inside the room, I spin in the empty space, convincing myself that it's my mind spinning and not the room. There's nothing here.

Where did it go?

Old curtains hang at the windows, ratty and torn in diluted shades of blue, but that's the only thing in the room.

Bare floorboards covered in a light littering of dirt stare up at me, the particles lifting into the air from my disturbance of their resting place.

Pushing my feet to move back into the corridor, my chest tightens and the ribcage cracks, crushing the organs beneath.

I look around the house, combing through every inch, marching towards the living space.

Nothing.

No furniture, just my suitcase sitting alone in the center of the room.

Old wallpaper rotting and peeling hangs on the walls and a mirror caked in a century worth of grime takes center position over the fireplace.

What the hell is going on?

Trepidation filters into my bloodstream, the unhealthy tremble bites into my fingertips with the need to itch the rushing of my own blood pumping manically through my system.

I'm losing my mind. Swiping my hand over the mirror, a reflection looks back at me, but it's not one I recognize and it's not until I lift my hand to clear more dirt that it confirms it's me.

Tapping at the back door gains my attention and Max beams at me through the glass at me, holding up two plates.

Waltzing towards him, I open the door and take one of the plates.

"Where has all the stuff gone?" I ask, almost panicked.

His brow quirks and he looks over my head into the space behind me.

"What stuff? Your suitcase?"

He pushes past me into the house and then stops in the living room when he notices my suitcase is right where we left it.

"It's there." He points.

Well done, detective.

"The furniture, Max!" I snap, waving my arms around. "It's gone."

I grab his arm and frog march him to the room where—when I arrived—had dead flies and dried blood-covered mattresses.

Kicking open the door, I open my hand to gesture inside.

"What?" he asks, small lines creasing his forehead.

"Where's all the mess?"

"Evi, you're not making any sense. What the hell are

you talking about?"

"This place was a mess. There was furniture and…"

"It's been empty for years. It was a crime scene. They used a crime scene clean up. All furniture contaminated with blood or other fluids got destroyed and anything left was kept in the basement."

Thud…

"Evi?"

"Where did it happen?"

He stiffens. "Why would you think I'd know that?"

I don't.

God, what the hell is happening to me?

"How did you find out about this place if you lost your memories?" he suddenly asks me.

Exhaling hard, I don't know whether to laugh or cry.

There is something building inside me like a surging sea and it is becoming too powerful to contain.

"I got a box from my mother to open on my twenty-first birthday."

My back hits the wall behind me and I slide down until my ass hits the floor.

"She was released from prison and wanted me to have the house."

"You know why she was released and when, right?" he asks me, drawing his bottom lip into his mouth.

My head tilts up to him. The plate of food I was holding is discarded on the floor.

"No. Time served?" I shrug.

Breathing through his nose, he drops down, placing his plate next to mine.

His fingers stroke out and tug a stray strand of hair behind my ear.

"She had cancer, Evi."

Had. Past tense.

"Had?"

Tilting his head, he drops to his ass and takes my hand
in his.

"She got compassionate leave because she was dying."

She's dying.

"That was three years ago."

My eyes snap up to his. "What?"

He nods, confirming what I thought he said. "It was in
the papers."

"No." That's not right. A wicked ache ebbs in the very
pit of my stomach.

Images attack my mind, firing like bullets, obliterating
everything I know to be truth.

My gaze drops to a scattering of small scars in half
moon dents around my wrist. **From her**.

*"You don't have to do this, Evi. She had no right to ask
this of you."*

*"It's fine, Mom." I look into the eyes of the woman who
has raised me for the last nine years, patting down her arms
and reassuring her to let me do this. The fabric of her cash-
mere sweater is smooth over my skin.*

*The voices haunt me inside my mind, whispering to me
about her.*

I need to do this, to give myself the closure.

*Her brown hair with specks of grey wisp from the bun
she has neatly constructed on the top of her head. Worry*

lines crease around her mouth, making her look older than she is.

Fragile hands stroke over my face.

"You're a good girl, Evi. She didn't deserve you."

Feeling a twinge of guilt for putting my adoptive mother through this turmoil bites at my conscience but it doesn't outweigh the intrigue, the overwhelming need to see my real mother, to ask her why.

Turning back to the nurse, I signal that I'm ready with a tilt of my head. She nods her head in return and leads me down a corridor.

Medical staff buzz around like bees from room to room, and from open doors, soft cries and beeping machines of other patients not quite as far gone as my birth mother leak out.

I didn't like hospitals. They stole my identity and left me empty.

Blue sterile walls, endless and cold, lead all the way down to a room at the bottom of the corridor. All on its own away from everyone else.

The place they take you to die is no more than a cupboard.

Pushing open the door, the nurse rests her hand on my arm. "Are you sure you want to go in alone?"

I'm always alone.

"Yes."

They had assured my adoptive parents that my birth mother was too weak to move, let alone do anything to hurt me.

They didn't account for loose lips though, and just the very sight of her cuts me just as deep as glass could.

There are no windows inside; the heat hangs in the air, concentrated and smothering, compressing down on me.

The walls look dirty in the dimmed lights. Grey rather than the white they actually are.

Machines beep and an accordion-looking machine pumps up and down, emitting a breathy whisper as it does.

The woman lying in the bed with tubes going into her hands and up her nose doesn't look familiar to me at all.

It almost makes me feel more lost in my own skin.

There's nothing I can relate to in her features.

She has a pale complexion, her skin thin like paper, the veins beneath green and on show, threading all through the film covering her bones. She doesn't have hair anywhere. No eyelashes or eyebrows.

Cracked lips whisper incoherent words.

Dazed eyes flicker open and shut.

There are tears building and leaking from the corners of her eyes, light brown eyes, the outline round to my almond shape.

"Evi," she croaks.

The room begins to dim and a coolness breezes over me despite the heat moments before.

Death has entered the room to take her away for her sins.

Closing the gap between the bed and me, I look down on her, waiting for her to evoke some emotion inside me, but there's nothing.

She's dying, but it's like a stranger dying. I can't find the right response inside me to care. It's simply missing.

I don't know her. I owe her nothing.

She doesn't know me.

I don't know me.

She whispers my name again and movement draws me to her hand turning over, her fingers wiggling.

Does she want to hold my hand?

I can do that, feel her hold on me, let her stroke over the steady thump of my pulse, the pulse she tried to snuff out.

Slipping my hand down towards hers, my body stiffens when her fingers, much stronger than anticipated, clutch hold of me in a death grip.

Her strength pulls me towards her, brittle nails digging into my supple flesh, breaking off and tearing the skin.

She's whispering something, her face void of any love. Any guilt.

Her fingertips are going to fuse with my bones if she tightens her hold any more.

I want to push her off me but her words send me spiraling into despair, her hushed tone-spilling lie after lie.

She's lying.

She's lying.

"Stop. You're making yourself bleed."

Max's voice penetrates the memory. Looking down at my arm, I've scratched at the tiny moon-shaped scars there and blood sits under my nails.

"I'm losing my mind." I shudder.

"No, you're not."

Nothing makes sense. I want to go back to the memory and focus on what she said to me. *If that was even real.*

If you stare so far into the darkness, maybe the darkness starts staring back at you.

"I need to talk to Garret," I tell him, scrambling to my feet.

His posture is rigid and he hasn't moved from the floor.

"Max, please. Take me back to your house so I can get my cell phone."

The ride back is like being sucked into a vacuum.

Neither of us are speaking.

My gaze keeps drifting to where he's sitting, thinking of last night when I was riding him like a rodeo bull right there.

The tension is palpable inside the small confines.

I roll the window down to let some air in and to have some sound other than my own pulse drumming in my ears.

What must he think of me knowing I have Garret?

Slut. Dirty Evi.

"I don't regret last night." I word vomit into the heated space between us, wishing my words got sucked out the open window before reaching his ears.

I don't regret it, but what if he does?

His sigh is weighted and troubled. Little pinpricks stab at my heart, waiting for him to say something.

One, two, three, four.

"Being with you could never be a regret. I wish it had been somewhere else and under different circumstances. You're not single, Evi, and your heart may be here, but your head is out at sea. I want to be the lighthouse for you so badly."

"I feel a *but* is coming?" I whisper.

His head swivels to look over at me. "But you have a boyfriend and I don't know where that leaves me in your life."

"I want you in my life."

That's all I know right now. The thought of leaving here and going back to my life where he doesn't exist physically causes pain.

"Then I'll be in your life," he promises, flittering his gaze between me and the road ahead.

And then we drift back into silence until he's pulling to a stop.

He gestures to the shop.

"I'm going to call the energy company to get the power on at your house and I'll bring some bulbs and things for when we go back."

Handing me a key to his apartment, he smiles tightly and nods for me to go ahead.

Opening the door, I locate my cell phone and Facetime Garret.

The music sounds, signaling it's ringing, and then his face appears after I contemplate hanging up.

"I'm so glad you got in contact," he tells me, like he's talking to someone he met on a business trip.

"We've been worried, Evi."

Moving to the couch, I sit to relieve some pressure from my feet, the cuts on the soles sore and oozing.

"Who is we?" I ask, confusion like static in my head.

"I spoke with Dr. Holst," he announces, and the old

clutches of shame drench me.

"What did he say?"

The corners of Garret lip curl back, showing off his perfect-shaped white Hollywood smile. He paid for that smile, there's no doubt.

"Just that you took off."

He's being careful with his tone. I know him well enough to know something is bothering him.

Did Edward tell him about what happened at the lake house?

"Did you go there?" I ask.

"I went and retrieved the box you left there."

The box that revealed who I was, only the memories of me seeing my mother years before are so real. *Too real to be fake.*

"Did my mother die?" I ask, my arm beginning to tire from holding the cell phone outstretched in front of me.

I prop up my cell on the coffee table and fold my arms over my chest.

"Evi, what are those marks?" he says, with the authority of a white coat telling me to take my medicine.

The red welts around my wrist appear angry. "That doesn't matter."

"If you've hurt yourself, it matters."

"It was nothing. Stop avoiding my question, Garret."

"What question was that, Evi?" he asks in such a calm, cool tone that it annoys me.

People pass behind him and the phone keeps jerking in his grip.

"Where are you?" I ask, changing the subject.

"Where are you?" he repeats, and I shift on the seat.

The front door opens and Max comes inside, placing a bag on the dining table.

"It's going to take a couple of days before they can get anyone out to reconnect the power," Max says.

"Who is that?" Garret asks, and the air stills along with Max's entire body.

"It's Max. He's the boy that used to live next door to me." *And so much more than that.*

"Why is he with you?" Garret's brow drops and he checks his watch and then nods to someone out of sight behind the phone.

"I'm with him, Garret. He's helping me."

Static breaks up my voice and distorts the screen and then all that's there is Garret, frozen on the screen with no sound coming from it.

We lost signal.

Dammit. Reaching forward, I grab the phone and slam it face down.

"I didn't realize you were on a call." Max's voice carries to me and I sigh, throwing myself back against the cushions.

"It doesn't matter."

He's just standing there like a spare part and guilt of making him uncomfortable in his own home itches away at my skin.

"I want to swim so bad."

"The school has a pool," he pipes up with a sparkle in his eyes. I must have spoken my desire aloud.

Excitement bubbles in my veins at the possibility.

"Accessible?"

Lifting a shoulder, he smirks. Going to the cupboard beneath his sink, he rummages through it and comes back holding some bolt cutters.

"Define accessible."

"Let's go." I jump up and let him lead the way.

CHAPTER THIRTEEN

DASTARD

The school is a small building, in the center of greenery.

There are boards at every window, graffiti sprayed in technicolor, creating words and pictures over them.

The wild has begun to take back the land. Weeds and moss crawl up the walls like a virus.

"This isn't what I had in mind," I cringe at Max who's broken the lock on the gate and is pushing it open with a nail-biting screech.

"It looks like shit but they didn't drain the pool and some locals hooked up a generator to keep the pumps going and the lights on. Trust me."

He grins and my stomach flips over in response.

This is going to hurt me.

He's going to hurt me because I already can't bear to think about leaving him, but I know I can't stay here in this town.

There's nothing here for me but more darkness, more confusion, more pain.

Walking across broken pathways and around the main building there are some smaller structures.

My breath hitches.

Lights shine from a classroom window above a door and I can already see the shimmering of the water reflecting out of the cracks.

"Why do people bolt the gate if this is here?" I breathe as he pushes the door open and steps inside.

Chlorine assaults my nose and sticks in the back of my throat.

"Just to try and deter teenagers from coming in and ruining the place."

The water moves like it's dancing to unheard music.

Tiles adorn the entire floor that borders the stretch of water, expanding at least forty feet.

Stripping off all my clothes, I push the pile of fabric back against the wall and dive straight into the blue depths.

The weight of the water pushing against my body brings a peace and calm to my mind.

Moving my arms, I glide through the water like I was created to live within it.

I swim the full length before breaking the surface and

gobbling down some air to relieve the burning in my lungs.

Biting my lip, I offer Max the biggest grin. "This is perfect."

His face mimics mine. "Yes, it is."

Splashing at the water, I tease him. "Come get wet with me."

His hearty chuckle echoes through the room, bouncing off the walls and hitting me straight in the groin.

Taking his t-shirt in his grip at the back of his neck, he lifts the material from his body in one swift movement, dropping it to the floor and thrusting it towards my pile.

Kicking each boot from his feet, he unbuckles his belt and jeans and slips them down his legs.

"I hope the Wilsons don't decide to come for a swim," he jests once he's standing stark naked.

I want to ask who the Wilsons are but my lips can't form words.

His heavy cock hangs semi-hard, jutting out from his hips, the muscle down his abdomen a pointing arrow right to his dick.

Strong, generous thighs hold up his mammoth frame.

He's extraordinary to look at, built in a way I've only seen in movies.

"Do you work out?" I find myself asking, breathless, a mischievous simper etched on my lips.

His lashes flutter, his eyes sizing me up as the corners of his lips curl and a hot flush creeps up my skin.

"I do a lot of yard work for people and try to be active when possible."

Well, damn. If yard work can create muscles like that,

every man should get out and dig the shit out of their gardens.

I'm so busy gaping at him and fucking him senseless in my mind that the splash of water and him disappearing below the surface shakes me.

His distorted form slinks towards me. Reaching out, his hand wraps around my ankle, pulling me under and wrapping me in his arms.

We break the surface together, giggling like teenagers without a care in the world.

The clear drops ping from his lashes, his whole face lighting up as we lock eyes.

I'm caught in his headlights and can't move, can't breathe.

This nervous, exciting energy zaps through me.

The essence of desire heats between my legs, and even though I'm balancing on a knife-edge right now, I advance on him.

My lips brush over his, the cold beads of water bursting over our joined mouths.

Pulling away, I stare at him, waiting for a signal that he wants this too.

A vein pops out in his neck, the pulse pumping fast.

Lust and something unreadable crosses his features before his hands tighten around my back, pulling me further into him.

His head rests against my forehead, his eyes fluttering closed.

"Evi," he whispers.

Drawing my lower lip between my teeth, I bite down

to prevent myself from saying anything that may break our spell.

"Are you going to leave me and go back to Ian?" he asks, clenching his jaw.

I know he means Garret and that he knows it's Garret not Ian, but I don't correct him.

I don't know what I'm going to do.

I'm stumbling through life right now, trying to find something solid and stable to cling on to.

I never imagined in all the darkness and horror of my past I'd find a crack of light bleeding in.

Max is the most breath-taking soul I've ever been in the company of.

The raw need inside him to take care of me, the way he looks at me; it's not just two adults wanting each other, it's so much more.

It's like we've been waiting and searching for each other's souls this whole time.

I'd never felt complete because I wasn't.

I know it's not normal to feel this way about a person so soon but I'm not normal, my life isn't normal.

Can two souls love each other before ever meeting?

Can they wade through the dusk to bathe in the dawn together?

"Do you believe in soulmates, Evi?" he asks, as if reading my thoughts.

He doesn't wait for an answer, instead he keeps speaking in soft tones that stroke over me like a lover's touch.

"My soul has known yours before we were put here on Earth and it will love you long after we leave it. Whether you stay with me or leave me to go back to your life, I'll find you again. I promise.

I'll hold on tighter and love you harder than any pain you've ever felt. All you'll ever feel is me loving you, showing you that in chaos where our souls grew, wild flowers flourish.

We're the wild flowers, Evi.

Unpredictable, untamable, and unstoppable.

I know you don't remember us and we were kids back then, but our bond was forged so long ago that it can never be broken. I know you feel it."

I do.

Crushing my lips over his, I writhe my naked flesh against the wet planes of his body, desperate to get closer, to lose myself to him, soar in his bliss until there's no coming down from him.

Hands explore until all caution is lost and we're bucking against each other, hungry with need so intense the water appears to heat from our burning friction.

All the strings keeping us restrained snap and fall around us like the embers from fireworks, igniting in our minds cracking and popping in an array of colors.

My legs wrap tightly around his waist, feeling the bulging head of his cock prodding and searching for entry.

We're moving, his body pushing us through the water, and the liquid glides around our bodies until my back hits the edge of the pool and Max's large hands drop to my waist, lifting me until my butt sits on the edge.

My legs part either side of Max's head, droplets bead and fall down his perfect face, heat blazing in his stare triggering a rapturous burn in my pussy so severe I moan and rub my hand there.

Moving my fingers away, he wraps his arms around my thighs and tugs me to his face, his lips fluttering over my needy opening, dipping his plump, hot tongue deep inside before bringing it up to tantalize my clit.

Leaning back on my hands, my hips rotate and writhe against his face, the small sprinkling of growth he has on his cheeks creating a magnificent chafe against the supple skin there.

Arching my back I push myself harder against his tongue.

He's feasting on me like I'm his last meal before a lethal injection. Savoring, devouring, agonizingly teasing until my dam breaks, my body pulls taut, and my knees close against his head, trapping him and prolonging the harmonious climax.

My skin is feverish and my heart is chasing the blood through my veins as I spasm violently before returning to a simmer.

"You're everything I see when I close my eyes," he confesses.

"So damn fragile in the height of pleasure. I want to see you release like that every day."

Me too.

My pussy throbs, the fluids inside trickling out from my orgasm.

I didn't know women could come until I saw it once in a porno film.

Pulling himself from the water, his arms tighten and

flex, the veins popping from the skin and making me groan.

What is it about those freaking veins in a man's forearms?

I scoot backwards to give him room to maneuver himself between my now fully extended legs.

His attention on the ruby slit he just had his mouth all over causes my nipples to harden even more, wanting the same attention.

With just a look, it feels like he has his hands and tongue all over my body, sending pleasure shivers racing through my blood stream.

His heavy presence leans over me, barely touching but feeling everywhere.

His hard cock slaps against my thigh and my pussy throbs, needy and hungry, wanting to gobble it up.

Teasing me with his lips, he places feather light kisses over my face and then bites my shoulder, tasting my flesh, his hands cupping and squeezing my tits in his grip, the thumb flicking over the peaking buds.

My head spins with filthy need and I almost beg him to put his cock inside me but he anticipates my need and drops his hand between my thighs, pushing two fingers through the folds until they disappear inside me. Reason, thought, everything but pure passion seeps out of me through my pores, leaving me a fiery flame, sizzling and hissing.

My lips pucker and I moan as I grip onto his arm and ride his fingers, enthusiastic and wanton.

His breathing burns over my skin, his eyes boring into

mine, riding the wave with me.

My pussy contracts and grips onto him as my lungs seize and my toes curl.

Every muscle constricts and sparklers glow behind my eyelids as a ripple of pleasure pulses through me.

"Yeah, let me have it all." Max groans, moving his fingers from inside me and nudging my thighs with his knee, prying my knees to part, his hard dick pushing against the swollen entry, forcing himself inside.

Reaching up, I cling to his body, pulling his lips down to mine.

Thrusting his hips forward, he enters me farther and farther until we become one person and melt into each other.

Our hearts thud frenziedly against each other's until we're just one pulse.

Strong strokes of his palms embracing over my body, lifting and caressing, turning us until I'm on top of him, his back to the floor with me sitting over his hips, his cock penetrates so deep I call out in rapturous desire.

His hands grip my hips to the point of pain, and it's delectable.

We move in unison, a dance between two souls seeking the sweet release into blissful eruption.

My movements increase with our panting and I drop my fingers between my legs to massage the needy bud there until we both topple over the edge of insanity and come together.

CHAPTER FOURTEEN

DEATH

Not moving is good right now.

My legs are weak and shaking and my heart is still racing inside its confines, despite having been just laying here in Max's arms for the past ten minutes.

His own body lifts and falls with exertion.

I'm waiting for the disgrace, the shame to slam into me, but it hasn't yet, and I beg my soul to not allow it in if it does come knocking.

"I'm starving," I announce, and we both chuckle, his body lifting mine with the force of it.

"That's because you run every time I try to feed you."

Lifting me from his body, he helps me to my feet and keeps hold of my hand.

My heart flutters like the trapped wings of a bird in a cage that's too small.

I know the wings will get damaged, but the fight to be free is worth the bruises.

With each step we take towards our clothes, I feel like I've boarded a rollercoaster, the teasing climb to the top, the flurry of excitement and that exhilarating fall, twisting, turning not knowing what's coming.

I don't want to get off yet.

He looks back at me over his shoulder and I see a thousand questions in his eyes. I'm at the mercy of them.

Don't ask me.

I don't know the right answer to give you.

His probing gaze caresses every inch of my being.

He knows my fragility and he tells me with every look, every touch, that if I was to turn into dust in a strong breeze, he would seek out the pieces and make me whole again. **Try at least.**

Can he be real?

Slipping his legs into his jeans, he leans down to fetch my clothes and his nostrils flare when he slips my top over my head and accidently brushes my nipple.

It's endearing that only minutes after being inside of me, he can react to a simple touch.

Giving me a lopsided grin as he drops to a knee and helps me into my bottoms, he places a delicate kiss on my mound before covering me with the fabric of my clothes.

My skin is sticky and my hair drips down my shirt

creating a wet patch to form.

My stomach grumbles with hunger and I want to go back to his place and eat in bed, then hide beneath the covers and pretend we're just two fools falling hopelessly in love.

I would never have believed anyone telling me something like this happens so fast, but the facts, the way I feel can't be argued with.

Trying to tell myself it's just sex, just a fling, is incomprehensible.

I found him when I so desperately needed something to anchor me.

"Let's feed you." He breaks into my thoughts and pulls me into the now.

The sky is a dark blanket sprinkled in stardust.

The breeze whistles, gentle and soothing, picking up leaves from falling trees and swirling them around our legs.

Creatures sing to each other and the dirty shame still hasn't invaded my mind. My skin.

"Shit." Max growls, dropping my hand. "I must have dropped the keys from my pocket." He jogs back towards the pool house and I find myself walking along the main building towards where we came in.

Ghost voices appear and fade in my mind; broken pieces of memory.

Like an apparition, I see Miss Bloom, younger, with a smile plastered on her face.

This was *my* school.

"Come on, Evi. It will be good for you to catch up. We

have a test next week."

"My parents won't allow it."

"I'll call them."

The images and voices dissipate as fast as they appeared and a crying sounds out; *it's a baby.*

"Found them," Max announces, holding them up in the air like they're a prize.

"Can you hear that?"

His happiness fades and he looks around, his body stretching to his full height and grabbing hold of me, placing me behind him.

"Hear what?" he asks, his tone deep and menacing. He's searching the trees and every darkened corner.

"The crying, Max."

Sadness clouds his features as he turns to face me. "It's just animals or something in the brush."

I know it's not out there but inside my head.

I'm losing my mind and grappling for normalcy with him is futile because there's so much still locked away that I can't access and there's so much he's still not telling me.

"I want to go back to the house."

"You mean the apartment?"

Shaking my head, I turn from him and walk towards his truck. "No. My old house, Max."

I sense his wince and hear his sigh.

Jogging to keep up with me, he slips his hand into mine, entwining our fingers.

"Tomorrow, I promise. Let me take you back to the apartment, and get some food in your tummy."

Grinding my jaw, I cave, hungry and tired.

"Tomorrow then."

His mouth sets in a hard line and he tilts his head to signal our agreement.

The drive back is filled with a comfortable silence, the throb between my thighs a pleasant reminder of everything that transpired earlier.

His words were so beautiful and heartfelt.

No one has ever said things like that to me before.

He makes me feel like I'm thirty feet tall and nothing can touch me.

Garret fades farther and farther from my thoughts, and as much as I try to pry into the time we've spent together in moments like that with Max, I keep coming up empty.

The night we spoke about the box at the lake house explodes into my mind like a bubble being blown and then popped.

Just like that, the picture fades.

I'm going to have to tell him more. About Max. About me and Max.

Garret has always been there to talk me through things, but like Max, it's becoming clear he has been keeping things from me too.

My mother, for one. I met her.

The box containing the letter from her isn't the first time I learned about her.

Is it the first time I read it?

Why would I suppress those memories? Urgh. Nothing makes sense.

It's so murky inside my head and so frightening being

lost inside my own chaotic mind.

I'm adrift, the balance of sanity and insanity is slipping farther from me.

I can't grip hold and keep myself from slipping under and being dragged deeper.

"Did Luke's family ever mourn him?" I suddenly ask from nowhere.

I wasn't even thinking about him.

Gritting his teeth, Max shrugs his broad shoulders. "I suppose."

"Where is he buried?"

"Christ, Evi. What does it matter?"

It doesn't.

Sensing I'm not going to drop the subject, he speaks again.

"His mother worked two jobs to keep that family afloat. She had three daughters and him. His dad got injured at the plant and couldn't take care of himself, and that woman was strong. She took care of it all.

Luke was a little bastard. Treated her like a maid and an ATM."

"Did I kill him?" I utter the words, already fearing I know the answer.

His neck snaps so fast to look at me, I almost get whiplash for him.

"No, Evi."

Thoughts of Daniel pitter-patter into my mind.

"There's this boy at the lake house. He was the neighbors' kid. Nineteen. He drowned in the lake."

His brow knits together. "Did you know him well?"

Did I?

"I don't think so." Weariness seeps inside me and my eyelids feel heavy.

Resting my head on the window, I let the vibrations of the wheels on the asphalt lull me.

That sneaky creep is out there again; I can feel him everywhere in here.

My skin prickles with awareness of my audience. Why can't he watch porn like most boys his age?

If I go and tell his father what a peeping tom he has, he will deal with it, but it doesn't stop him creeping around my windows.

He's only a couple of years younger than me. I don't even know why he still comes up here with his family.

I've seen them together. All they do is argue and separate into single activities. Dr. Edward likes to golf, while his wife gives his credit cards a workout.

Daniel and his brother sometimes fish, but Leroy mainly plays his video games while Daniel comes slithering around my place.

"I see you!" I bark, as I pull a t-shirt over my freshly cleansed skin.

The hot shower had soothed the ache Garret had left after not giving into my offer of phone sex.

He's a selfish prick when it comes to sating my eager sex drive.

Lifting the window latch and shunting the panel up,

breaking twigs sound from beneath it, and I know if I stick my head out, he will be right beneath the glass.

"I know you're out there, Daniel. Why don't you come inside?"

I offer, with an inviting tone lacing my words.

Not really sure why I'm letting him inside, I decide to play cat, and he's the mouse.

The room is hot and the AC needs replacing; another job Garret promised to do and still hasn't.

Walking towards the bed, I sit, and smirk when I hear the front door squeak open.

His black hair falls like melting ink off his head, covering his entire forehead.

He's bigger than his waif-like brother.

He plays lacrosse and it shows in his shoulders and arms.

Maybe this won't be such a waste after all.

"Don't just stand there. Your greedy eyes can't stop watching me through the panes of glass. What is it that summons you to spy on me, Daniel?"

His brows rise and a rosy glow highlights his cheeks under the florescent lights in the corridor to my bedroom.

The t-shirt he's wearing pulls taut over his chest muscles, a soccer slogan emblazoned across the center.

A red hoodie hangs, draping on his arms. Shorts sit loose on his narrow hips and the zipper is low.

I know his grubby little fingers have been tugging and tossing over his fat stump of a penis.

He must barely be legal. I can't quite remember his actual age.

Do I want to know? No.

I slide up the bed so my feet point towards him and my elbows rest just on the pillows at my head.

Heavy breathing carries across the room and his chest heaves, giving away his excitement.

He will no doubt come in his pants before getting closer.

Flicking his hair to the side, he wipes a hand over his head and fists them, letting them drop back to his sides.

The protruding bulge is pronounced in his shorts and I take back my stubby thought.

Dropping my knees, I let my legs part to expose my clean-shaven pink slit to his greedy eyes.

I can almost taste his desperate urge to get closer.

"Do you want to touch me?" I torment, letting the words slide over my tongue like satin sheets on virgin skin.

He moves into the room, bold for a heartbeat, but then his feet falter at the edge of the bed.

All those times watching isn't the same when I'm laid out in reaching distance.

"Daniel, do you want to touch me?" I ask again, scolding him with my lips. I'm crossing a line, and seeing his father on the lake maybe awkward after this, but he had it coming, and boredom and insomnia can play tricks with morals.

"Yes. More than anything." His jaw goes slack when I move my hand to the plump mound.

"Then do it," I dare, unsure if he even has the balls to back up his perversions.

His mouth opens but words fail him. He takes a step towards the bed, reaching out with inexperienced fingers.

Amateur, unworthy brat.

I kick his hand away, and he startles, his eyes expanding, making his features appear much larger than I thought.

I shake my head. "Not with your dirty little fingers. Use your tongue."

The smell of bacon creeps into my nostrils and my bedroom fades.

The aroma invades my subconscious and I jar awake.

I'm in water*. What the hell?*

The lake. I'm still at the lake house in the middle of the lake, too far from shore.

I've swum past the marker.

My body tires and my legs kick more softly until they stop and I begin sinking.

It's so cold, my skin feels like ice; I'm freezing. Fighting to reach the top and drag air into my lungs, I can't swim.

My arms betray me and stop trying.

My mouth opens to scream and cold lake water floods in, drowning me. I'm dropping faster and deeper and everything is getting darker and darker.

I brace for one last effort to fight to the surface, but something twists around my foot.

Tugging and yanking to free myself, the grip around my ankle firms and I drop my head to see what it is.

"**NO!**" I scream, and sound thunders out of me and my body launches forward.

I'm falling, and with a thud, I hit hard floor and light explodes into my eyes as they shoot open.

Warm air radiates around me and I'm not wet or drowning.

I'm not at the lake house, but in Max's apartment on the floor, having fallen from the couch.

His feet pound towards me from across the room, cautious, worried eyes assessing me as he bends to help me up.

"What the hell happened?"

I shake my head. "Nothing."

"Evi?"

Cradling myself, I rub down my arms. "A bad dream."

His expression transforms his face from delicate perfection to rugged excellence.

Pity shines from his eyes as he asks, "Do you want to talk about it?"

I don't need pity. God, if he knew the things I did.

Those moments in the dream with Daniel are vivid and solid in my brain.

That happened, the sexual act, and the disgrace caused the drowning dream to penetrate my memory.

"No." I answer him bluntly when I realize he's still crouched next to me, waiting for a response.

"I made some bacon sandwiches."

I did smell bacon.

He takes my hands and helps me stand. My ass smarts from falling hard on it from the couch.

"Your phone has been lighting up," he tells me with a cautious tone.

He hasn't broached the topic of Garret; not that we've had any time to.

The dream lingers in my head and acid burns in my gut.

I let him touch me so intimately like it was nothing. Like it was playing cards, catching a movie.

What night was that?

Max places a plate in front of me and pulls a chair for me to sit in at the table. "Thank you."

"Wine or milk?"

"Is that the only options?"

"Tap water." He grimaces.

Placing my hand over his, I give him a reassuring tilt of my lips.

"Milk will be perfect. Thank you."

After going to the kitchen to fetch the milk and a plate stacked with bacon sandwiches on for himself, he takes a seat next to mine and pours the white liquid into my glass.

"Thank you."

"Do you want to talk about your dream?" he asks before taking a huge bite of his sandwich, demolishing half of it in the single bite.

I finger the bread on my plate and linger my stare on the condensation dripping down the glass.

"Do you think you can dream your memories?"

His jaw flexes with each chew and I become mesmerized with the way his throat bounces as he swallows.

"Some memories never fade and instead hide so deep that it takes separating yourself from reality in order to seek them out," he answers, watching me.

That kind of makes sense.

"Do you think someone can be evil just because of the blood in their veins?"

Placing his hand over mine, he squeezes so tight the bones crack underneath and he almost chokes on his food, lifting my hand and kissing it.

"Shit. I'm sorry."

Why? It didn't break anything.

"Do you not believe that there's only so much evil you can live with before you stop living with it and it begins to live inside you?"

I turn my chair so it faces his, and he cups my cheeks, boring his dark orbs into me.

"You're a victim, Evi." He breathes the words, believing them.

"I'm no-one's victim, Max."

I'm here, I'm breathing, I'm alive.

Where are they? Dead and gone.

Shaking his head, sorrow torments those beautiful eyes.

"You're a victim. A victim of your own tormented thoughts. You're a good person who had bad things happen to her."

A tear leaks from my eye and I want so badly to swipe it away, but Max is moving towards me, his lips press down kissing away the watery tear in its tracks, taking it inside himself to take some of the damage for me.

"Even the purest of us still create a dark shadow," I whisper.

His grip tightens. "Then let's live in the shadows together."

He pulls me into his lap and I snuggle into the crook of his neck, breathing him in. He must have showered when he brought us back here because he smells of the citrus shampoo that I know is in his bathroom.

"Please eat something."

He picks up my sandwich and hands it to me.

I'm aware that his cock is growing in length beneath my ass and my appetite changes from one hunger to the next in a blink of his chocolate-colored eyes.

Biting my lip, he smirks and shakes his head.

"Eat your sandwich, and then if you finish it all, I'll eat you," he teases, slapping his palm across my thigh.

It's the most erotic thing I've ever felt.

So simple. So fucking hot.

I want him to slap my ass, my thighs. Spread me open and slap my pussy.

I stuff the sandwich into my mouth, biting off a chunk and pushing the stray rasher of bacon poking out into my mouth.

"Yum."

His chuckle only ignites my need more.

CHAPTER FIFTEEN

DEMON

Heavy limbs lay over mine and I don't want to move them or grind on his knee for some friction.

I just want to lay here in the harmony of our breathing.

After he ravaged me in the night, he pulled me into his arms and cradled me like he was frightened I'd flee, but in all the years I've felt a piece of me was missing, I know now I'd been searching for that stray part of me in all the wrong places because this is where I was supposed to come to find it.

The sun trickles through the window and kisses over the bed, teasing us with its affection.

Max groans next to me and muffles something incoherent, and I manage to wiggle from his hold and tiptoe down the stairs to use the bathroom.

After relieving my bladder, I rinse my hands and then go to the kitchen to make coffee.

I already sense his movements before seeing him.

"Why are you not still in bed?" he asks against my ear, wrapping his arms around my waist and nuzzling into my neck.

"I want to get a good start on the day." A grin creeps over my face being in his embrace, as if we're two carefree people just falling in love and living life without a care.

I don't want it to end.

Turning in his grasp, I place my hands against his chest and welcome the slow drumming of his heartbeat.

"I can go alone if you need to open your shop."

It's only now occurring to me that he has a life, a business, and here I am invading his world and keeping him from his responsibilities.

"I'm the boss, so don't worry about the shop."

I take a minute to take in the apartment again and the information about his mom not going back to work after his dad abandoned them.

"What made you open a hardware store?" I ask, brushing my lips across his chest.

He looks off into the space above my head in thought.

"I dropped out of school early and did odd jobs here and there, and then my grandfather passed away, leaving me some inheritance. I knew if I didn't invest it I was going to be a waste of space like my father, coasting through life and blaming everyone but myself for my problems." His chest deflates a little at the mention of his father.

"I had mom to take care of so I asked a friend to help me with some investments, and a couple of them paid off and made me a good profit." Dropping his head to look at me, he continues.

"I bought this place from an old timer, eighty-five years old and who had lived in this town his entire life, his family going back generations to the people that first built it. The place was a dive, used as a storage dump for an antique shop. That was what my shop was before Mr. Strafford passed away."

His expression hardens, speaking of the death of the old man.

Was he close with him? Did it upset him?

"It was going into liquidation, so I got it at auction for a fraction of the cost it would have been and renovated."

That's incredible.

He mentioned only being twelve when my mother went on her rampage so that only makes him a few years older than me, and yet he's established himself in the community and set up a business and home.

What have I accomplished?

"Come on. Let's get some coffee with breakfast at the bakery across the street."

Sugar for breakfast? Damn, he really is perfect.

The heat outside hits me like a brick wall.

Air is restricted in the smog and I almost miss the rain when the beads of sweat glisten over my body.

People mill around the shop windows and come and go in various doors.

The town that seemed like a ghost town at night is alive and busy in the day.

The door closes behind me and Max offers me a breath-stealing grin.

"Ready?" he asks, holding his hand to me.

Yes. **A thousand times yes**.

My hand just clasps his when a woman steps from a nearby car and I recognize her straight away as Miss Bloom.

Sniffling, she takes a few steps towards us and then stops, her eyes flitting to our entwined hands.

Her face reddens and she licks her lips and purses them.

"I wondered if I could talk to you?"

She's looking at me but I'm not sure if she's actually addressing me.

An uneasy tremor rocks through me and my paranoid mind tells me there's more to her and Max then he let on.

I risk a quick glimpse up at him and all the happiness from this morning has evaporated from his posture.

His jaw clenches and then his lips curl back in a snarl.

"She doesn't need to hear what you have to say just to make yourself feel better, Riana. How fucking selfish are you?"

I haven't heard Max swear before now, I don't think, and it seems cold on him, unnatural even. He really holds something against this woman.

But in a sense, he is right. Why does she even care? Everything happened.

It's done, no matter how bad she feels that she didn't prevent it.

"What do you want to say that could mean anything to me?" I ask, truly wanting an answer that will justify her seeking me out, unless this was just a ploy to see Max.

"Sorry." She speaks on a broken choke, like it's obvious and should mean something to me.

Screw her apologies.

My hand drops from Max's and I take the few steps toward her until I'm close enough to see the crinkles around her mouth, the hardship of her life spiraling off in a different direction then she had planned.

She's running on empty, broken within, like me.

"Why didn't you do something? Tell someone?" I ask, curious of her answer.

Her mouth pops open forming an o shape.

Her lips vibrate and tremble like she has words to speak but can't form them.

"If Max told you about me, why didn't you do more?"

It's a genuine question.

I don't know what she did or didn't do, only that it hadn't made any difference.

Her arms wrap around her waist to hold herself up.

"There wasn't proof. If I told my superiors and was wrong it could have ruined my career."

She really just said that.

Kids know no different. If I was born into abuse, how

would I know what was right and what was normal?

Teachers are supposed to notice, look out for and protect us when we can't do it ourselves.

Max told her what was happening to me and she must have believed him enough to take pity on me and try to give me a birthday, and yet it wasn't worth her career.

My safety, my sanity, my innocence.

And in the end, look where she ended up.

"How's that career working out for you, Miss Bloom?" I taunt.

A fat, salty drop leaks down her cheek.

"Keep your sorry for someone who can use it, because It's just more weight on my already heavy shoulders and I'm losing the strength to keep it up."

My feet adjust to turn away from her when the world tips on its axis.

The back door of her car opens and a tiny child gets out.

The world around me slows and noise ceases to exist, all except my heart that beats so loud I fear everyone can hear it.

Can the world just pause so you can feel your own soul being ripped from within the essence of your being?

Thud...

My lashes blink, watching in agony of the implications of who she is and who she belongs to when she takes off running towards Max, a chortle pinching her chubby cheeks and her arms outstretched.

I'm bound to the moment by the unsettling welling beginning to build inside me.

No.

"One thing lead to another."

Max's arms open and he crouches to collect the child in his embrace.

A thousand tiny needles dance there way over my scalp and my breath is subconsciously punched from my chest.

I battle for an anchor to steady me in this moment.

I feel like I've been dragged from a dreamful bliss and dumped into the rude awakening of reality.

He didn't mention them having a child.

Rage and disgust snap and fight for control of my actions.

Do I have a right to be upset?

Blinking, I know tears shimmer in my eyes as I observe the similarities.

In the child who has eyes the same as the man holding her.

In the logical part of my mind, I tell myself that these things happen all the time, but in the maddening, lost part of my mind, anger and disappointment take hold.

Desolation settles over my skin like dew seeping into the pores when I hear her giggle.

Echoes of past laughter funnel through my corrupted thoughts and push my body into action.

Wordlessly, I take the keys hanging from Max's fingers before he can stop me.

His calls sound around me, setting fire to my insides, but I leave him with the ashes.

Jumping into the truck, I key the engine to life before

skidding out of there.

The radio's noise fills the cabin trying to distract from the betrayal I suddenly feel.

"Debris left on the tracks has been blamed for the devastating crash that claimed three hundred and thirty three lives."

I slap my hand against the radio button to turn it off, sick of the news presenter's monotone voice.

No one cares, woman.

They're dead.

Whatever caused it, they're just freaking dead.

Everything hits me at once, a tsunami of emotion tumbling over me, angry waves swallowing me up before pounding me against the shore.

Tears fall in a torrent of angry sobs.

The road blurs before me and my hands shake against the steering wheel, the overwhelming need to release everything from inside me is like a dam bursting and a life of uncertainty and grief crashing through it.

I don't understand what it is I want anymore.

There's this desperate longing and an intense fear that nothing will ever free me from the dark hold of myself.

I'm crawling in the dark with no torchlight to guide me in the right direction.

I want to hold my breath, swallowing the life I'm sleepwalking through and fade into the abyss.

CHAPTER SIXTEEN

ANGEL

Jumping from the truck, I don't even switch the engine off, I just leave it sitting idle as I spill from the seat into the fog of the morning heat.

Sweat drips down my back and the house appears smaller than it did yesterday.

Max's mother's curtains twitch and I debate going to her and asking her what she knows about everything that happened with my mother and family, and if she knows her son already has a child with a woman twice his age who used to be his teacher.

I guess my appeal would grow a couple of scales compared to that reality.

Serves her right for being a judgmental bitch.

My hands shake and I drop the keys trying to open the front door. Bugs crawl over the ground at the front step and I stab at them with the sharp edge of the keys.

It takes three attempts before I get inside and slam the door shut.

Giggles bounce around the walls followed by crying.

There's an overbearing buzzing inside my skull and everything is thick and heavy around me.

My legs buckle and I tumble like Alice down the rabbit hole.

Silhouettes of boys pass me, their face a blur, but they're caked in mud and carrying shovels.

A man, also distorted, an unnatural being rather than a human, enormous and imposing.

His outstretched hand beckons me and something inside me obeys without delay.

Fear grips me in its hold, its claws of unmistakable doom creeping around my throat like a vine of thorns, squeezing, scarring, infecting.

My feet want to dig into the ground and stop myself from being dragged into the punishing night when he opens the back door and steps outside.

I'm wearing just a vest and underwear, and the cold slithers into the bones and roots itself there.

Wind and rain whip at my small frame and the monster, with me in his grip, pulls me further from the house into the woods.

The trees seem to come to life under the darkness of the

night, grasping and moving, hissing with their arms.

Animals stalk and howl, and I know out of everything that should scare me, the monster who should be the one to protect me from danger scares me above all others.

Dirt squishes between my toes and lodges under my toenails.

I already know he won't let me bath this late so I'm going to have to sleep in the dirt and ruin my sheets, which will get me whipped with his belt tomorrow.

All of a sudden, he stops and launches me forward with no effort at all and I stumble, almost lifting clean from the floor, but land just as quick with a painful thump.

Twigs break underneath my body as I crumble into a big ditch-like hole.

Damp earth collapses around me and the hole I've fallen into is deep and deliberate, created by my brothers because my daddy would have commanded it.

"Daddy?" I whisper with a stutter as my teeth chatter.

The bones creak inside my skin as I shake, unsure if it's the cold or the fear making them rattle.

Acid bubbles in my tummy and I think I'm going to be sick, which I know will make him even madder.

What did I do to make him angry?

I run off the chores on my list that I have to do on Mondays and I completed them all.

I wasn't late home from school and I helped cook dinner, and I even went to my brothers when they ordered me to.

I cleared the blood from mom's sheets.

I was a good girl. I was a good girl, Daddy.

A sneer pulls up his lips and create fang-like shadows.

"If you tell anyone about her, I'll bury you both out here and no one will ever know. The bugs and worms will eat you alive and you'll feel it all, buried beneath the dirt like an animal."

His words are cruel and harsh and I know he means them.

Crying sounds out and his head whips back to the direction of the house.

I see mom holding something in her hands, cradled against her chest. She followed us.

I won't tell. I promise. I promise.

Raised voices penetrate through the haze and the dream-like memory evaporates.

Tell anyone what?

What is my mind hiding from me?

Everything hurts over my body and the taste of pennies coat my lips.

Crap.

I'm on the floor and must have hit my suitcase on the way down because it's turned over on top of me and my face smarts as I crawl to my feet and look in the mirror to see a cut on my lip and a bruise blossoming over my cheek.

I'm riddled with injuries and I'm so tired of being here.

Tired of hurting. Tired of fighting myself.

The rumbling of male voices signal from outside and I sidle up to the window and stare out.

Thud...

Two broad figures stand out in the front garden.

My stomach flips over when I recognize the unmistakable sound of Garret's voice.

Garret?

"She's not a well girl, otherwise I wouldn't be here. Now let me see her, please," he says to someone in front of him

"Where the hell have you been? You're supposed to be her boyfriend and yet you allowed her to come here alone?" Max's voice causes a jump in my pulse.

Max and Garret are here, together?

"I'm her doctor."

Shut up, Garret.

"What?" Max grits out.

Go away, Max.

"Not her boyfriend. I'm her doctor. Evi has had a psychotic break and I fear she's spiraling further into psychosis. I shouldn't even be discussing this with you," Garret grates, and the atmosphere in the open space around me becomes taut, closing around me in a throttling fog.

I'm not her boyfriend.

Psychosis.

"How did you know she was here?" Max asks, and Garret turns from him and looks over at the house.

I pull back and hide against the wall, terrified of being in the same space as him, as them.

What if what he's telling Max is true?

"Why didn't she remember that her mother died?" Max shoots question after question at him.

"She left her lake house and came here because she said her mother left her a letter and the deed. She didn't remember her dying."

Stop.

Stop it, Max. I scream internally.

"It's not her lake house."

What?

He's lying.

Stop pulling the thread, Max.

Stop it.

"The lake house you're referring to is a not a property Evi owns or lives in. She was staying at Greenfields Psychiatric Facility. It's up at Green Lake."

No. No. No.

"A mental hospital?" Max sneers.

"I can't discuss this information with you," Garret announces after already indulging Max's questions.

"Just fucking tell me! Is it a mental hospital?" Max roars, and a shower of goose bumps explode over my skin, my womb crying out to him, my yearnings flooding my system and wiping away the confusion.

Why do I have this sexual urge so powerful inside me?

Silence hangs in the air so deafening I want to scream out just to shatter it.

"No, it's not a mental hospital. It's a voluntary facility. A resort of sorts," Garret finally answers.

"A very renowned doctor owns the property and runs the facility and Evi chose to be there until recently when she fled with no explanation."

That's not true.

I live at my lake house.

This is a misunderstanding. Garret's just protecting me and feeding him lies.

A fist pounds on the door making me jump, but Max isn't finished.

"Why wouldn't she tell me all this?" He sounds broken, distraught, and betrayed.

It's all lies, Max. Don't listen. Go away from here.

The world I know feels so fragile, like everything is made of paper and a storm cloud has begun to trickle down upon it.

If I don't hold onto the balance, it will become a water-fall, turning everything I know to mush.

I count the seconds of their silence.

One.

Two.

Three.

I'm being swallowed up in the hush of their tongues and the need to swim, wash away everything bad, sharpens within me.

"Because she doesn't know what's real and what isn't, she creates a world and lives inside it."

I don't.

Do I?

What's real?

Pulling open the door, the gust it creates lifts my hair and tosses it over my face, sheltering me from both prob-ing sets of eyes that turn to me.

"That's not true, Garret," I whisper.

"Evi, it's good to see you again." He is speaking with a careful method, one someone would use to approach a criminal holding hostages and not wanting to startle or an-ger them.

Who is my hostage?

You are, Evi.

I just want to be safe inside my head, make all this go away.

My eyes creep over his form and my heart thunders.

He looks older than I remember.

"Why would you tell him those things?" I ask knowing, if it's true and we're just doctor/patient, he's divulged more than he should have.

Tears burn in my eyes but I don't allow them to fall.

"Because they're the truth, Evi. You moved to Greenfields after your parents' accident."

Thud...

My parents weren't in an accident.

Thud...

Were they?

Why hasn't mom been calling me?

Thud... Thud... Thud...

"I don't understand." The thoughts begin to hum like static.

"We're so sorry, Evi. Both your parents were amongst the dead."

"Did something happen at Greenfields?" he asks me, his forehead puckered and his gaze intrusive as he steps toward me, trying to placate me.

"You're ok, Evi. Just breathe." With his words, I realize I'm gasping for air and my chest is once again crushing my lungs.

A shadow creeps over me and blots out Garret and the world. Max's scent coaxes me back from the brink of passing out.

"Shh, just relax. I've got you, I promise."

"Nothing he says makes sense," I say.

Crying echoes in the back of my mind and I find myself smacking my hands against my skull to shut them up.

"Stop doing that," Max instructs, taking my hands in his.

The child of Miss Bloom's comes into focus in my thoughts and I pull away from Max.

They all lie to me.

They all lie.

His pupils flare and he holds his hands up in surrender, begging me with his eyes not to pull away.

Don't run, he tells me with just a look, but I'm being dragged into my own madness.

"I just need it all to go away. It hurts too much." I close my eyes.

"We're not creatures made to be alone, Evi. You left that place seeking something and you found it here. Sometimes the worst parts of our lives lead us to the best parts. Don't run from this. From your past. From us."

His words penetrate my soul and I want to believe him and let him make everything better.

"How could you be with her after she let this happen to me?" Tears trickle from my lashes and down my cheeks.

Miss Bloom didn't help me and yet he let her be with him.

His lips part and he searches for clarification, and before I give him some, realization dawns on him.

"The child is my sister, Evi."

What?

Crying resonates from somewhere behind me. I turn

to follow the sound but Max doesn't allow me to drift.

"The baby, it's my dad's. He lives in the next town over. He and Miss Bloom were together."

That bitch.

"But you said you two slept together."

I hate that she experienced him like that.

Shame waters into his eyes; it's the same look I see in the mirror every day.

"She didn't tell me until after. She was angry with him because he left her."

Oh God, she's a manipulative bitch.

"So, she used you to get revenge?"

Shrugging his shoulders, he looks heavenward and then back down to me.

"My mom doesn't know about Gracie."

Gracie, the child.

He could have told me all of this before when we spoke about her.

He's gazing up at me, waiting for what?

He appears so brittle in this moment, breakable, and yet I'm still captivated by him.

Taking a step towards him, I take his hand and entwine our fingers, his so much bigger than mine, and it makes me feel safe in the midst of so much uncertainty.

"I don't know why, but what Garret is saying isn't right."

Garret's sigh sounds from behind the protection of Max's body, which is creating a wall between us.

"Maybe you can just hear him out and see what does feel right to you?" Max says.

"I'm scared," I admit, my heart bleeding.

I need his arms around me to prevent me from crashing to the floor and being lost to my dreams, my nightmares, my insanity.

CHAPTER SEVENTEEN

MEPHISTOPHELES

G arret steps into the house, carrying a box.

The same box from the lake house.

I'd agreed that I'd hear Garret out and decide if I believe what he's telling me to be truth.

"It's not a lake house. It's a facility."

He places it down on the suitcase and opens the lid. It's ratty and torn like I remember.

My hands wring together and an itch burns my flesh, akin to a thousand ants invading my pores and crawling under my skin.

"You remember who I am?" Garret asks, his expression hard but stoic, and I scoff, rolling my eyes.

Of course I know who he is.

"You're my therapist and boyfriend." I falter on the sentence.

We are that, right?

"I have been your therapist for three years. I've never been your boyfriend, Evi. When your birth mother died, you repressed all memory of the entire passing. You didn't recall meeting her, visiting the hospital, or even knowing her."

"Why?"

How can that be? Isn't that what I've been searching for? A link to my past to give me some answers?

I try to ignore the *"I've never been your boyfriend, Evi"* because I don't know if he's just saying that because it's frowned upon or if our relationship is all fabricated by my loneliness.

"It could be the trauma of the situation. You came away from her bedside with injuries." He gestures to my hand and I instinctively lift it and rub at the half moon scars there.

Max lifts my hand and kisses over the marks, and my pussy throbs in response.

How can I even think about sex at a time like this? Thoughts of them sharing my body right here on the dirty floor has flickered into my mind like a flame, gaining strength the longer we remain in the room together. How damaged am I to even want that?

I take one step forward and two steps back.

"Why do I like sex and use people's lust against them?" I sense Max stiffen and the room grow smaller around us.

I've always garnered attention from the male population, but beauty is just a magic spell to hide the ugly. My beauty is all that people see; it's a shiny distraction used to blind people, and people use me because of it and I use it against them too.

Garret's jaw tightens as he appraises Max.

"It's okay, Garret. Just answer the question, please," I beg.

"Promiscuous sexual behavior can be commonly seen in various mental disorders such as psychosis," he tells me, his face unreadable as he looks between the two of us.

"So I'm crazy?"

"No, Evi. Not at all. You had a psychotic break. For someone who has been through trauma like yours, it's not uncommon."

"I want to know what's in the box."

Max squeezes my fingers to let me know he's supporting me and that I'm in a safe zone. I can handle whatever it is.

"You received this box when your mother passed away. It was her only belongings."

So not on my birthday?

Reaching inside, he pulls out some papers.

The news clipping that I read, and birth certificates.

I take them from him and my hand trembles as I flip through them, seeing they are my brothers' and mine.

And then my mother's.

Melanie Devil.
Mother: Ada Devil
Father: Nolan Devil

Pulling the next one to the top of the pile, cement solidifies my bones. My father's.

Anthony Devil
Mother: Ada Devil
Father: Nolan Devil

My hands loosen, letting the certificates flutter to the floor.

I drop to the ground, my hands wrapping around my knees just to hold myself together, scared I'm going to evaporate into the air to save myself from the truths that just cause more damage.

"They were brother and sister," I choke.

Flies invade my headspace and buzz their wings so loudly I place my hands over my ears to try and quiet the pandemonium.

Max fumbles around, picking up the papers and looking over them.

Don't look. Don't see what I am.

His sad eyes droop and his beautiful face turns to look at me.

Don't look at me like that, Max. Please, just let me be normal.

"I want you to breathe in and out for me, Evi," Garret tells me.

He moves closer to me and kneels in front of me.

Grasping my hand from my head, he turns the palm and places two fingers over the pulse in my wrist.

"Count with me, okay? And with every number, I want you to exhale."

"One."

Du dum. Du dum. Du dum. Du dum.

"Two."

Du dum. Du dum. Du dum. Du dum.

"Three."

Du dum. Du dum. Du dum.

"Four."

Du dum. Du dum.

The rise and fall of my chest matches the gentle thrumming of his fingers tapping over my pulse.

Tears build in my eyes.

"Is there a letter?" I ask, and Garret releases me and nods his head in confirmation.

"I'm not sure you should read it though. It's a lot for you to take in for one day."

I need to read it. I need to know what it says. Does it read how I thought it did, or did I create a whole script for that too?

Lunging forward, I take the box and pull out the letters. Plural.

These weren't there before, were they? There are loads of them, all addressed to the house I grew up in with my adoptive parents.

Pulling one from the envelope I read her words.

Evi,

I know what you did. I know what you did. I know what you did. I know what you did. I know what you did. I know what you did. I know what you did. I know what you did. I know what you did I know what you did. I know what you did. I know what you did.

I know what you did. I know what you did. I know what you did. I know what you did. I know what you did. I know what you did. I know what you did. I know what you did. I know what you did. I know what you did. I know what you did.

My brow crashes over my eyes and my nose scrunches.

What the hell is this?

I tear open another letter.

Evi,

I know what you did. I know what you did.

And another and another.

Evi,

I know what you did. I know what you did. I know what you did. I know what you did. I know what you did. I know what you did. I know what you did. I know what you did. I know what you did I know what you did. I know what you did. I know what you did.

I know what you did. I know what you did. I know what you did. I know what you did. I know what you did. I know what you did. I know what you did. I know what you did. I know what you did. I know what you did. I know what you did. I know what you did.

"What the hell is this?"

Silence.

"Where is the letter with the deeds to this house?" I demand, scrunching up the ones in my hand and throwing them to the ground.

Pity clouds Garret's face and I want to slap it off.

"Garret?" I push.

"There is no such letter, Evi."

Getting to my feet, I ignore the ache in my bones as I do.

I push my hand into my pocket.

"How would I have the keys?" I pull them out, holding them up.

Silence.

My head swivels from one to the other. Max's frown is so prominent on his head it transforms his face, creating creases around his eyes.

I drop my hand and look down at the bundle in my palm.

Thud...

I want to scream.

Run.

Cry.

Chase away this nightmare in the lake, swim it all away.

I'm losing my mind and they're just standing there watching it happen.

The bundle of keyrings in my hand is a collection of useful tools. *There's no key.*

Carrying my feet to the front door, I swing it open, the latch giving away with a gentle push.

Wood that once was nailed across the lock is dislodged.

You don't need a key to get in; I must have broken the wood away and broke in.

No.

I remember not being able to get the key in the door and having to re-try.

Do I even own this house?

"So whose house is this?" I pin Garret with my glare.

"As far as I could determine, it belongs to the bank."

Oh my God.

How can I have lost my way so badly?

I'm decomposing in here somewhere and this isn't real. I'm a ghost haunting the space, surely?

"Evi." Max's voice thunders through my haze.

I want to call to him.

I'm fading, save me, but it's all too much and my lips won't form the words.

Can he even help me? My soul is so heavy it's crippling me.

"What happened to my parents?" I look up at Garret, ready to hear the truth about what set this all in motion.

I try to cling onto an image of them, an emotion to

strike inside me, but it's behind a sheen, a window keeping me from experiencing what lies on the other side.

"They were on the express train that derailed and killed nearly three hundred passengers."

No. No. No.

Pain bleeds into my heart and the wings of the trapped bird inside flutters madly, trying to break the confines and fly free, escape the agony his words bring.

The article in the papers. The news on the radio.

Dark shadows creep around my skull. A sinkhole inside my chest opens and sucks all the sanity into it.

Flashes of myself on a campus play like a movie before my eyes.

Not happy, but a content me, studying and training.

"I was in school. A swimming scholar." I exhale. Oh my God, how could I have just erased that from my own life?

"We should arrive at four-thirty. Are you coming to pick us up at the train station, darling?"

"They were coming to visit me." Gasping for air, I pinch at my skin to prove to myself that I'm living, because this feels like dying.

I've been walking in a daze of falsehood. Nothing is real.

I'm a swimmer. I have a coach who thinks I can be Olympic material. Coach Russell.

Oh God, Coach Russell. And yet I deleted him like an eraser over paper, expunging half the story.

Nausea swirls unrestrained inside my stomach, burning up, setting my chest ablaze.

My lips pucker with half-formed questions. Answers. Regrets.

Blood congeals like tar in my veins, struggling to keep a steady heartbeat inside my ribcage.

I was living in my sorrow, a storm that kept raining down on me without mercy, and I couldn't pull myself through it.

I got so lost, so broken when they died.

"You had an emotional break, Evi and I recommended Doctor Holst's facilities for you to take some time and get more full time help that you needed."

Doctor Edward.

So he's real?

"I need to go there."

"Where?"

"The lake house," I say urgently.

I need to see for myself that it's a delusion created from my own sorrow to try and protect myself from experiencing the pain of it.

"Garret, please!"

He brings his cell phone from his pocket and runs his finger over the screen. "I can take you there on the fifth?"

That's three days from now.

"I need to go now." I look to Max pleadingly.

"I will take you."

I want to apologize to him.

Explain that I don't want to be crazy, that being with him wasn't part of my illness.

That I care about him and feel more for him than I have ever felt for anyone. But words stick in my throat like glass and all I can do is offer him a broken smile as I swipe the mourning falling from my eyes.

"I need to pack some things and then we can go today."

"I wish you would wait and let me come with you, Evi. You still have so much we have yet to delve into. Unlocking your past has always been what we were working towards in our sessions."

"I need to see the lake, Garret. Come with us."

Do this for me. Don't make excuses and just come with me, goddammit. I'm your patient if nothing else, and I need you to come with me.

"I can meet you there tomorrow?"

Tomorrow.

"Thank you for coming here," I tell him honestly.

"Are you sleeping, Evi. Did something happen at Greenfield? Was it Daniel's disappearance? Do you know where he is?"

Daniel?

Yes.

No.

What does it matter now?

"He died. Suspected drowning, a year ago."

His face twists in confusion. And I know I'm wrong. That isn't what happened.

I don't want to hear the sounds coming out of his mouth anymore.

"He disappeared two weeks ago, Evi."

No. That's incorrect. I need to see Edward.

"I will see you tomorrow, Garret."

"It's Doctor Osmond."

"You don't allow me to call you, Garret?" The name Osmond doesn't ignite any familiarity.

His mouth twitches into a half grin and he rubs a hand at the back of his neck.

"I try to keep things as professional as possible for your own benefit, but you have always played with your own set of rules."

He places a hand down on my shoulder and thoughts of him flutter like a butterflies wings bringing new beauty with each stroke.

Memory after memory glimmer behind my eyes.

"I want to fuck you, Doc. Is that normal?"

"Lust is a common trait amongst us all, Evi. Don't fight it or be ashamed of feeling it. Just learn to harness it better."

"I dream about you. We're a couple and live on the lake so I can swim all day and you can write your medical journals."

"It's an escape for you but unhealthy to see me that way. You know that can't happen. Do you want to discuss why authority figures are appealing to you?"

"I already know, Doc. Daddy issues."

"Tell me what you remember about your birth father."

"Nothing solid, just a daunting, hopelessness encasing me whenever I let him conquer the spaces in my mind. He steals the light."

"That light is yours. No one can take it from you. It's safe to think about him in here."

The floor creaks, shattering the hold Garret just had over me as Max's feet stomp across the room and he takes my hand in his.

"Let's get some things packed and hit the road. Bye, Doctor Olmond," Max growls

"It's Osmond," Garret says.

And then the heat of the day is back, burning through my thin clothes as Max helps me into his truck and slams the door closed.

The keys are still in the ignition and guilt trickles over me. I shouldn't have taken his truck without asking.

"I'm sorry about Gracie. Your father and that witch, Miss Bloom."

The atmosphere is tense and I hate how different everything feels now compared to our happy place this morning.

"None of that matters. None of them matter. You matter."

I matter?

"I know there's more to our childhood then you're willing to share and more than I'm able to remember, but I do feel it, Max."

His hand slips into mine but his eyes remain fixed on the road stretching out before us.

"I know you're who I belong with," I add and close my eyes.

Sleep is scarce and scattered and my body is drained and exhausted.

I don't want to dream; the memories torture me there, but my eyes close anyway.

CHAPTER EIGHTEEN

ADVERSARY

*A*ll the news channels are playing the same thing.

Water drips from me, creating a puddle on the floor of Coach Russell's office floor.

"We don't know anything yet, Evi. Try not to panic, okay?"

I'd been doing laps all afternoon. My time had been slower today than most days because I was distracted knowing I was picking up my parents from the station and they were going to spend an entire week here.

Our relationship isn't a typical one. I've never really been a loving person, and although there's a fondness and gratefulness towards them, I'm not like most girls I came to *know here at school, but my mother knows this and accepts what I do have to offer.*

Being disjointed in the world isn't easy.

I didn't make friends at first and still only have one who is more an acquaintance than a real friend, and only that because she's on the swim team.

A towel is placed over my shoulders and one of the other girls from the team tells me to come sit down.

I don't want to sit down. I want to get changed and go about my day.

Mom will call and I will know that they're okay and they still need me to come pick them up.

Leaving the room without a word uttered, I sense the heat of Coach's gaze on me as I make my way to the changing room.

I need to speak with Garret.

Days pass. I was given a hotline number to call for hospitals but Garret has offered to take care of things for me.

The world has become misty, overcast, and I'm wading through, trying to be normal.

What am I if I don't have them?

A rap of knuckles on the wooden door of my room thunders and startles me. I already know doom stands on the other side.

"We're so sorry, Evi. Both your parents were amongst the dead."

Dead.

Gone like everyone else in my life, my past.

A stabbing pierces into me and I'm taken aback by the sorrow that knocks the wind from me.

How do people cope through such pain? I know it's not a new ache because with their death comes a sting so sharp it's like I'm being reincarnated over and over just to be punished with this heartbreak.

I vanish inside myself, I stop going to class, I stop going to training. I just stop.

Days creep into weeks and everything becomes less vivid, like I'm seeing the world through smudged lenses.

Sleep evades me and hunger is meaningless, thirst a trick of the mind because eating and fueling your body is only for the living, and I'm not living.

I'm an apparition of someone who longs to be whole.

Despair is so exhausting.

I long for someone to take it all away for me so I can breathe again.

My appointments with Garret are the only things I keep going to.

The brown carpet reminds me of mud.

He doesn't have a receptionist, just a waiting area I know I have to wait in until he opens his office door and summons me inside.

His demeanor is always strict and professional and coming here is the only time I feel something other than the crushing despair.

Crossing my legs to add some pressure to the pooling between my thighs, I cross my arms so my nipples scrape against them.

Licking my lips, I take a seat in the chair opposite him, where I always sit.

When he takes his seat, I uncross my legs and let them part so, if he wanted to, he could see straight up my skirt.

I forwent panties today so the ruby slit hiding at the end of the tunnel of my thighs is there for him to see.

"Are you sleeping?"

Boring.

"Eating?"

Boring.

"You look like you've lost some weight since you were here last."

"Checking me out, Doc?" I toy with him but he doesn't play my games. His face remains stoic and not once have his eyes dropped to the prize I have for him.

"I would like to suggest you spend some time at a facility not too far from here so you can return to school after break."

Break is here?

"Dr. Edward Holst is a specialist in the field of…"

His words fall flat and that garnishes my attention from his cock area. Draping my stare up his body, I pause when I see he's looking where he shouldn't be.

An explosion of lust bursts into me, dripping out from my needy hole. Can he see the glistening on my thighs?

He stands abruptly and goes over to his desk that sits along the back wall.

He picks up something from there and comes back over, gesturing with his hand, a card between his finger and thumb.

"We can continue our sessions via Skype while you're there."

Taking the card from him, I sigh, disappointed that he didn't take the bait.

I've been trying to get him to fuck me on his desk for the last three years.

He's the only man never to cave to my approach.

I wondered if he's gay many times, but he never shares personal things about himself with me.

"I've made arrangements already for you."

The rumble of the engine easing to a stop arouses me from slumber.

Dribble coats my bottom lip and I swipe it away and stretch out the kink in my neck.

"Hey, sleepyhead."

My eyes adjust to see we're at a drive thru.

"I ordered you a burger and fries," Max says.

It's night time now and I wonder how long I must have been out.

Taking his order from a thin teenage girl at the window, he thanks her and places the bags in my lap.

"I thought we should stay overnight in a hotel and go to the lake house tomorrow morning."

I don't want to wait but he's probably right so I nod my head in agreement.

Offering a tight smile, he drives us a few miles before pulling in to a motel.

"I can take you somewhere nicer if you want. I found this one on Google. It has a pool."

I'm already getting out of the truck.

Could he get any more perfect?

The sting of remembering my parents' death weighs heavy in my heart and getting to swim to tire me back out is exactly what I need.

Max goes to book a room and I venture over to where a stoop overlooks the communal pool.

Taking a seat, the smell from the fast food bags reminds me how starving I am.

Pulling a burger from the bag, I unwrap it and bite off a mouthful.

My stomach cramps when it hits the acid in the pit of my gut.

I keep eating until the entire burger is gone and a burp pops out just as Max makes his way over to me.

"Excuse me," I mutter, placing a hand to my mouth.

His lips quiver and then he's chuckling.

"Even your burps are cute," he teases, taking the bag from me and ushering me towards a room.

The room is basic.

A queen bed, small table, two chairs, and a bathroom.

Testing the bed, I bounce my butt up and down and try to avoid Max's eyes.

I know he must have questions for me, but how can I give him answers when I'm not sure what they are myself?

"I'm sorry about your parents," he says, and a shadow darkens the room as if grief is an entity and it's just entered.

"They were good people. Couldn't have children of their own and instead of adopting a newborn, they took me in. My father worked at the hospital. He was there when I was brought in and he said he knew I was sent to them." I shrug.

"That's why the adoption happened so fast, I guess." He moves to sit next to me, handing me a carton of fries.

"Were you happy with them, growing up?"

Abandoning the fries, I lie back on the bed and look up at the ceiling. There's a stain right above me and I'm curious as to what could have caused it. It's dirty brown.

"I've never been like everyone else. There was always something missing for me and I longed for something I could never sate. Hope and love have always eluded me. I feel different since finding you."

And that's the truth. He makes me feel like I'm capable of normalcy, love, a life.

"What are you hoping to get from going to this Greenfield place?" he asks.

I don't know.

"I need to see it, to believe it. The lake house, the lake… it's all so vivid it's hard to believe that I could have fabricated something so detailed."

Sitting up, I crawl into his lap, my arms wrapping around his neck.

"Thank you for coming with me. For not leaving me when you learned how crazy I am."

I sense his smile and the shift in his body. His arms encircle me and he holds me to him.

"I knew from the first moment I met you that you were mine and I was yours. It's hard to explain how I knew being so young and naïve, but I won't let you go ever again. As long as you want me, I'm yours and you're mine, in all your crazy colors."

A laugh trickles out of me and my hands fist in the fabric of his clothes.

Thank God I have him.

Don't let me go, Max. Ever.

"Do you want to go for a swim?" he asks against the skin below my ear.

Yes.

"I want to make love to you first."

Only in the ecstasy of sex when the throb of your pussy pounds to the exact beat of your heart do you know you're with the one.

I was no longer lost at sea.

Max was anchoring me, floating with me, teaching me that through tragedy and disarray, unique bonds form and when the tide gets too rough and the waves too high, your soulmate will guide you back to the shore.

Everything Garret divulged took its toll on me, but here I am in Max's arms and I'm breathing.

Coming out on the other side of my own madness seems possible in his embrace.

I don't want to swim the bedlam away in my head, because in his arms… it doesn't exist.

The shower pounds against my body and the patter of its

drops massage my scalp.

There's been a constant thud inside my skull since I opened my eyes this morning.

Small cuts scattered all over my body from various falls and runs through the brush sting as I wash soap over my body.

My hand stills when the tiny half moon dents on my wrist touch the pads of my finger.

"I know what you did with her, Evi. I know what you did."

The shower curtain pulls back and startles me.

Max's naked, impressive form climbs inside, cocooning my body with his.

"I thought we could save water?" He smirks.

Sure you did.

CHAPTER NINETEEN

ROUGE

Green as far as the eye can see, and it's a reprieve from the grey/black asphalt we've been staring at for the last hour.

I like it here, close to the water. I can almost smell it in the air.

If I don't own a lake house here then I may buy one.

My parents' life insurance will see that I never have to worry about money. Knowing their life came with a price tag makes the money feel dirty somehow.

"Here we are," Max murmurs, gesturing to a white wooden sign stretching out at least six feet in width and five feet in height just in front of a black iron gate that's open.

The driveway is long and leads to a stunning house. Edward's house.

Thud...

I know mine is just through the trees. I'm out of the car before it even pulls to a full stop. My feet kick up dirt as I race through the trees.

The lake ripples in greeting and my feet stutter to a stop.

Thud...

There it is. It is here.

Crunching sounds behind me and I turn. "It's here, I knew…"

Words fall from my lips and Leroy stands there, sneering at me.

"So you came back then? Is Daniel with you?"

Daniel is dead.

"Daniel drowned in the lake."

His eyes flare and his gaze turns to the lake.

"How do you know that?" he asks, shocked, his legs moving towards the small pier.

Jacqueline is standing down by the edge and I point to her.

"Go ask your mother. She knows he drowned."

Leroy's posture stiffens. He folds his arms over his chest. Scars in white lines like a ladder cut into his flesh travel the length of both forearms. I've never noticed those before.

"Are you drunk?" he bites out.

"What? No."

He quirks a brow and looks between his mother and me.

"That's Jacqueline. She's a patient here, not my mother."

Thud...

"No. She's Daniel's and your mother."

He flinches backwards as if my words struck him.

"Daniel isn't my brother, Evi. I can't stand that asshole. Are you off your meds?"

I don't take meds.

Edward's form appears from the tree line and it's all familiar and yet totally terrifying.

I'm staring at strangers.

"Evi, welcome back." He points over his shoulder.

"I found your friend." Max who has joined him and Leroy.

"Edward, who is Jacqueline?"

"She's a permanent resident here at Greenfields."

"Not your wife?"

His lips press together and he exhales.

"Evi, why don't you come inside?"

No.

"What's this? This is mine, right?" I ask, pointing up to the smaller version of his house.

His head bows in a slow nod.

"It's the cabin you were staying, much to the upset of Leroy who wanted this accommodation." He jests.

"Whatever." Leroy Huffs bending down and swiping up a leaf that he tears into pieces.

"This isn't a mandatory facility, Evi, so some of our residence like you have cabins and are free to come and go. We just ask that you inform your care team when you do leave and sign back in when you return."

207

"She's a crackpot. She needs an institution, like I said before. Ask her where Daniel is," Leroy scoffs.

Thud...

"Do you know the answer to that, Evi?" Edward asks.

No.

Yes.

Leave me alone.

"I want to go inside?" I ask, but it's not for permission; my body is already half way up the path.

The door gives way under my hand and I push inside, letting the door shut behind me.

Visions assault me, broken and cracked, of me and of Daniel, the night I remembered inviting him in.

"Not with your dirty little fingers. Use your tongue."

He gains a confidence that was absent moments before. Grabbing my ankle, he shoves my legs farther open and leans in to taste me.

Regret and humiliation burns away all the adrenaline in my veins and I try to pry my legs closed.

"Get off me, Daniel!" I demand, pushing his head away from me.

His hands grab mine and he looks up from between my legs, his mouth forming a hard, bitter line.

"Don't fucking tease me, Evi."

I squeeze my legs together against him. His rage grows and he uses his elbows to prevent me.

"Stop it, you asshole!" I flay, trying to free myself from

the stupid position I've put myself in.

Daniel was at Greenfields because he had issues with his temper and broke a fellow Lacrosse player's nose.

His parents are wealthy and sent him here so he didn't put a mark on their reputation.

"Get off me, Daniel!" I screech, pinching, punching, and attempting to kick him.

I don't want this. I shouldn't have invited him inside.

This is my fault.

He gets to his feet and I use the chance to scamper across the bed, but he's fast and grips me around the back of the neck.

He forces me face down onto the bed and the covers bunch around my mouth, restricting my breathing.

He lets lust control his actions, his grip tightening in my hair.

I don't tell him no anymore because it doesn't matter; he will take what he wants anyway.

I don't beg him not to because I can't breathe and I'm dying.

"You're a fucking tease! A dirty little whore who thinks she can play with me. Well, you can't."

The intrusion as he enters me burns and old images of past forced sex assaults me, dragging me under.

Air fails me and I'm suffocating in the fabric of my being. He's stealing all my color.

The virus inside me stirs and takes over, dragging me into a void of nothingness.

Void of beauty, void of love, void of hope.

I wake, coughing and sputtering, as oxygen blisters into

my lungs.

"You fucking deserved that, Evi," he spits.

I want to scream but my demons don't allow it.

I know better than to make a sound, to protest.

On shaky legs, I make my way out of my cabin and down to the lake, and before the water has even tickled over my toes, Daniel is behind me.

"Cleansing away your sins?" he jeers, amusement in his tone.

Images of another boy, another time, expand and pop in the forefront of my mind.

I'm bending, picking up a boulder, the world's blurring the images, becoming one.

I spin, hitting him with all the strength I have. The crack is like a symphony.

His eyes widen and the pupils expand as a swell of crimson essence blooms and begins to gush like a waterfall down his face.

His lips move but the words are incoherent.

My heart races in my chest as he staggers forward.

The small boat we take out on the lake is tied next to the pier and I quickly move to grasp hold of Daniel's arm and guide him to the boat.

He falls with a gentle shove inside of it, his head colliding with the wooden plank used as a seat.

The snap cracks the still air and excites me.

That broke his neck.

"You fucking deserved that, Daniel." I mimic his words and untie the rope bounding the boat to shore. I give the boat a push using all my weight and hop inside, sitting on Daniel's

back, using the paddle to get us far enough out that no one will see us.

When all that accompanies me is the static air and the motionless water, I use the paddle to smash a hole in the side of the boat, letting water pour in.

Jumping into the water, I pull down on the side of the boat, helping it along to fill and capsize.

Daniel's body hits the water with a splash and then it swallows him up, sinking him into his dark, deep depths.

The boat follows him under, cleaning away the blood.

The torment of his act leaves my soul twisted and my heart scorched, the ash settling in my eyes and distorting the beauty the world has to offer, all the healing tainted.

All that was possibly now seems pointless and unachievable because anger and disgust has infiltrated my bones, my marrow, my soul; it's all I see.

I swim fast, strong strokes, and when I leave the water, I'm someone new.

I killed him.

I killed Daniel.

He raped me.

He evoked old thoughts of another time. **Luke.**

I need my memories back. I need to know what I am, what I've done.

Staggering back outside, Doctor Edward and Max are waiting for me, but Leroy and Jacqueline are not in sight.

The water beckons and whispers my secrets to me.

"How are you feeling, Evi?" Edward asks, and Max is moving towards me, wrapping me in the safety of his arms.

"I did something bad," I whisper against his chest.

"It doesn't matter."

My will spasms, my fight between victim and perpetrator rage like a war inside the fragmented pieces of my cranium.

"I need to go to Garret."

"Okay, then let's go."

"I can help you if you're willing to stay and let me," Edward tells me, and I wonder if everything that transpired between us was made up in my imaginary world.

I don't trust my own version of things and don't want to talk to him.

I need Garret; it's time to go back. Go back to the beginning.

CHAPTER TWENTY

ACCUSER

The room seems more colorful than I remember.

Books line bookshelves and there are plants thriving in pots situated on shelves and stationed in the corners.

Is that to make the air cleaner?

Garret agreed to see me at his office instead of at Greenfields and now I'm so terrified of what we will discover, everything around me feels like it's compressing against my temples.

A shiver moves through me, causing every hair follicle to rise in awareness.

My mind prowls into the dark corners where shadows

213

hide the memories of my past.

The rasp of Garret's fingers flexing before tightening on the arm of the chair he sits in opposite me causes a stir in my stomach.

His tall, dominating presence when he's in doctor/patient mode quells any argument I'd usually throw his way when he wants me to open up about my past.

I'm breathing heavily from thoughts of all that's transpired since I was last here with him, in his office.

He glances at me, creeping his gaze over me, seeing right through to the marrow of my bones.

"Tell me what you remember from that night, Evi," he orders me.

But I'm fighting the pull and shaking my head in response.

He uses my name with affection, his tone caressing the syllables, confusing me further.

The dynamics have shifted so much from patient/therapist that I don't know what's right and what's wrong anymore.

"You need to do this. It's time," he pushes, offering me a reassuring nod of his head.

His almond shaped orbs like a cat's prowl and probe, beckoning me to succumb.

But I don't want to. Instead, I want to beg him not to make me remember, but I know he's right. It's time.

The sleepwalking has become too dangerous and the information from other people just doesn't add up.

The waves of memories haunting me don't make sense.

He won't let me avoid this any longer. I don't want to

avoid this.

I need to know. I need to know who I really am.

Fear seats itself in the forefront of my mind.

What if you don't like who you are?

"Remember. Tell me what happened," he demands, his voice hardening with authority.

My hands ball into fists as my heart thunders like a battle drum inside the prison of my chest.

Thud... Thud... Thud.

I focus on the balls swinging and clashing on the small Newton's Cradle that sits on the table beside me.

Closing my eyelids, I search the murky depths of my thoughts, wading in farther and farther.

Mirages flash before my senses.

Disconnected, partial images, like swimming from dark water farther and farther toward the shoreline where the water clears and what lies beneath becomes unblemished, solid surface. Color. Sound. Smell.

My insides seize and sorrow swells in my chest. Icy drops tap dance over my skin.

"Where are you, Evi?" Garret asks.

I'm there in the past, within the body of the old me, gasping for air in cracked, quivering breaths. Small, broken. I'm only a child, staring up at an endless black that spans before me.

"Tell me?" Garret's voice anchors me.

The sky expands before my pupils, a dusting of stars battling to shine through the thickening darkness of the night. I'm so cold. Too cold; my body heavy, damp. The concrete beneath me offers no comfort.

"I'm lying on the ground. I'm outside."

"Where outside?"

My observation flitters to the structure made up of discolored wood and glass.

The terror, too horrifying to indulge the memory, battles to seat itself in my mind.

Strangers whispering, haunting my thoughts.

I know this place. I wish I didn't.

"It's my home. Our home. I'm in the yard of my old home," I choke.

Tangled strands of my wet hair stick to my head, hardening like cement. I lift my hand and the small digits show I'm young; a child.

My hand drops with a heavy thud.

The night has turned colder than any before it, blanketing me in an icy chill.

"I'm dying," I whisper.

I will be a frozen ghost if I don't get inside.

My body is weakening with every shallow breath I take in.

"You're okay. Breathe."

My body spasms, causing pain in my solidifying joints.

My brain is willing me to move inside to the warm, but my limbs don't feel like my own and they refuse to obey my commands.

"I can hear something," I mutter.

It's faint but solid, so I cling to it.

"What do you hear, Evi?"

Hushed voices are sounding from an open window.

My mouth peels open to call out to whoever it is, but

it's only wasted breath, too quiet to be heard by anyone but me.

"I can't feel my legs. It's so cold."

There's a throbbing in my stomach but it doesn't compare to the expanding pit inside my chest.

It's too much pain. I'm screaming internally, wishing it would all end.

"You're okay. Keep going, Evi."

I don't want to. It hurts too much.

Hot tears pool and leak over my eyelashes, and I fight the memory so I don't have to face the crushing ache.

The pain opens in my ribcage; a black pit of sorrow, empty and consuming.

Reality floods in; the smell of Garret's aftershave and the warmth of his office. I'm back in the room with Garret, not dying on the cold concrete floor. Lifting my hand, my perusal takes in the size of my palm. I didn't die. I'm a woman now.

"What are you feeling? Why did you come back, Evi?"

I shake my head, fighting him and myself mentally so I don't have to dissect this expanding ache.

"Don't make me feel it," I beg.

"Feel what? What is it you're feeling?"

A gasp escapes my lips as the pain from the memory washes over me like black rain, saturating me in its oily residue. I'll never get clean.

"What is it?"

"Grief." I grip my chest to make sure there's a heart still beating in there.

It's crippling, desperate sorrow, and it's drowning me

from the inside out. I want to close myself off and fade into the heartache, never to resurface, but it's too late.

It's like I'm an intruder to the emotion. It's not mine to own. It's the little girl's who I abandoned when I forgot who she was.

Who I was.

"I'm dying!" I cry out.

Garret moves from his chair to kneel in front of me.

Grasping my hand in his, he squeezes hard, producing enough pain to show me this is real and not the memory I'm living in.

"You're not dying. You didn't die, Evi. You were saved. Go back. Remember."

His words cocoon me in their safety.

My lids flutter closed and I let the weight of my sorrow wrench me back there, the cold expanding over me like wet quicksand, swallowing me in the memory.

Footsteps slap against the wet surface around me and a boy's face appears, blocking the darkness of the sky.

"Someone is here."

"Who is it?"

My gaze is unfocused as I stare up at him.

His features are distorted, like I'm looking through a misty window. His voice as he breathes my name is familiar, though. I hold onto it, willing myself not to leave him.

"It's a boy."

"Here. Here!" His lips move, calling out into the night, desperation in his tone.

Other footfalls sound around me and a burst of sweet scent fills my nostrils.

"It's a woman's face now replacing the boy's. She's saying something."

"What is she saying?"

"She's alive! Get a paramedic out here now!" the woman shrieks.

Her warm hands caress the cold, tight skin of my cheek. Her calming voice holds affection I'm not used to.

"It's okay, sweetheart. You're going to be okay. Stay with me."

"Eleanor," I croak.

"Who's Eleanor, Evi?"

"Who's Eleanor, sweetie? Can you tell me where is she?"
Eleanor.

Other voices join hers, but my sight begins to cloud over and there's a humming in my ears.

"She's lost a lot of blood. We need to get her to the hospital now."

"I'm dying. Everywhere is numb."

"No, you're not. Stay with them, Evi."

"Did you find another girl inside? She's mumbling a name. Eleanor?" the woman mutters to someone out of sight.

Eleanor.

"No. Three males inside. No survivors."

My eyelids are too heavy; they're falling, pushing me under.

Eleanor.

Then there's nothing. The sky falls and swallows me into the obscurity.

"Go back to when you were on the ground and called out the name Eleanor. That's the same name you call out when you're sleepwalking. I want you to focus on the voices around you. Try to stay with them. Listen to them. Close your eyes and go back."

Thud... Thud... Thud.

"Did you find another girl inside? She's mumbling a name. Eleanor?"

Eleanor.

"No. Three males inside. No survivors."

"I can't keep my eyelids open."

"**_Stay with them, Evi._**" Garret's voice penetrates my thoughts.

Eleanor.

Eleanor.

"She's her sister." The boy's familiar voice murmurs so softly it's like the whisper of snow hitting the ground.

Thud... Thud... Thud.

What? No. I don't have a sister.

Wait. Eleanor.

"No."

My body jolts as if I've been struck by a thousand volts.

Memory after memory crashes into me, almost

knocking me to the floor.

"Eleanor!" I cry out.

"Who is that, Evi?" Garret asks, his brow furrowed.

"She was my sister, and the cause of it all."

CHAPTER TWENTY-ONE

DECEIVER

Evi

Eight years old

S creams tear through the house, coming from mommy and daddy's bedroom.

Lucian keeps coming out and disappearing back inside with towels.

The angry boom of Daddy's deep voice sounds out, bouncing around the walls and then crying follows.

Lucian comes barreling out of the room, his face as

white as the sheets on our beds. He has blood on his stomach and hands and I cringe at the thought of what that could have been caused by.

Dad's heavy feet pound the ground and the bare floor moves on the foundations.

Miss Bloom pops into my mind.

She will be proud of me for remembering that houses have foundations; it's a topic we're learning about in school.

Dad has gathered the boys in the kitchen and then they disappear out the back door and Dad nods his head toward mom's room, an order to go in there.

I duck my head and hurry my feet into mom's room and cower when he comes in behind me.

"Clean that up," he snaps at me and my stomach rolls.

There is blood and wet stains all over the bed.

What happened?

Noise squeals from the bathroom attached to their room and as I turn my head towards the sound, a snap resonates across my cheek and a stinging burn explodes over the same path.

He hit me, my head whipping to the side and my hair delayed, suspended in air before curtaining my face to hide my tears from him.

He always hates my tears.

Gathering up the bed sheets, I take them to the basement and load them in to the washer.

I'm not sure how those stains will come out of the cotton but I add bleach because I've seen Mom do that before.

It spatters and rushing water sounds out.

I tiptoe back up the stairs, hoping to stay clear of

Daddy's wrath and just go to bed.

My brothers enter the house with mud all up their shins and shovels in their hands.

What were they doing so late at night?

When Daddy turns his attention on me, I shrink and pray that I become so small I can turn into dust and be swept away.

He grabs my arm and pulls me into the night.

I'm in a hole that my brothers have dug, and Mom is staring at us both from a clearing in the trees.

She's holding something to her chest; the baby from her tummy.

Why can't I tell anyone about her?

Daddy leaves to go back to Mommy and I'm not sure if I'm allowed to climb from the hole or if he wants me to spend the night out here.

It's too cold. Please don't leave me here.

"Get in the house and clean the mud your brother's trodden in."

I scarper from the ditch; it takes me a few attempts, but by the time I make it, I'm alone, and I run as fast as I can so the trees don't swipe me up and tangle me in their branches.

It takes me over an hour to clean all the floors.

I've been able to tell the time since I was seven.

The big hand moves and I sigh, dropping the mop into the bucket and creeping on soft feet to my room.

Because everyone else has gone to bed, I was able to give myself a wash down with the mop water so I won't soil the sheets.

I hear crying, a baby's piercing scream through the night, and want so badly to go to her and comfort her.

The next morning, Daddy comes into my room early to tell me I have to stay home and help Mom today.

I don't mind; it means he won't be around so I'll get the whole day without him or my brothers.

Mom always sleeps through the day and the night so it's like she doesn't even exist anyway.

After making them all breakfast, they depart and I'm left alone.

The house always feels different when they're not inside and I want to call to Max when I see him through the window, leaving for school, and tell him to stay home and spend the day with me.

Crying coming from Mom's room distracts me though, and I miss the chance.

I see the back of his rucksack as he climbs onto the bus.

I know he will be looking for me and scared that I'm not on the bus.

He worries about me so much; he's the only person who has ever cared about me.

"Shh," I hear my Mom hiss and I move towards her room.

I softly push the door open.

A basinet sits in the middle of the room.

My feet creep over the floor and I wince when it creaks.

Mom stirs but doesn't fully wake.

Her pill bottles line the dresser.

She says she needs them because monsters don't let her sleep.

I'm not sure if she means the same monsters that don't let me sleep, the ones she lets hurt me.

As I reach the basinet, my stomach feels like it's falling out of me and hitting the ground.

The baby's face is wrong. She looks odd, her top lip is pulled up into her nose.

I reach in and move the blankets from her body, and her tiny feet bend weird and I think that may be why she cried so much last night.

I twisted my ankle once and it hurt for weeks afterward.

She begins to fuss so I scoop her up and cradle her to my chest; I'm so happy I have a sister.

I take her from the room so she doesn't wake Mom and make her angry; she can be nasty when she's mad.

I take care of the baby until Daddy comes home.

He glares at me for so long when he comes through the front door that I almost wet myself.

"Remember what I said," he warns, and I think back to the hole outside.

"I won't tell anyone. I promise."

"Not even that kid next door, Evi, or I'll kill him too."

No. Not Max. Never.

His words are the cruelest, most painful thing he's ever said or done to me.

Max is everything, and when we're old enough, we're going to leave this place. I'll take my sister with me and leave the rest of them to rot.

"Here's her milk. Read the instruction and make her bottles up. You're in charge of her feeds."

"Okay."

I'm good with Eleanor. I like taking care of her. Keeping her a secret from Max is nearly impossible but she's been here for three months and five days now and he hasn't guessed or asked about a baby.

Mom is useless.

Some days she will be present in the world and want to hold Eleanor, but for some reason, she calls her ugly and deformed and she blames Daddy.

They argue but they have always been that way and I ignore them most of the time, grateful they're hitting each other and not me.

I'm just putting dishes away after breakfast when Lucian calls for me and it makes me want to cry.

It hurts so much when he does those things to me and I feel rotten inside for days after.

Eleanor is still sleeping when Lucian is finished with me.

I sneak out the back gate and into the sanctuary of the trees.

When I get to the water, I breathe in deeply.

They don't come out here and the water cleanses me of their disgusting acts.

I hear movement behind and then the voice of Luke.

He's caught like a wolf in a trap.

All the times my brothers have forced themselves into my body.

The time I refused them and hit Lucian with a trophy he had won for baseball, Daddy had punished me so severely, I couldn't sit down or go to the toilet from my butt without screaming for a month. All anger and pain take over my actions.

I got better and learned my lesson with my brothers, but Luke isn't my brother, he's no-one; a horrid worm who thought he could taunt me. Well, he can't.

The boulder in my hand comes down on his foot, snapping the bone.

It feels good. A zapping sings inside me and I want to do it again. He's crying and cursing and I'm laughing.

"You're dead, Evi. I'm going to fucking drown you in that lake you love so much," he sobs, and I realize he may do that.

Daddy might get mad if Luke tells people what I did.

My heart skips when I see Max standing just under a hanging branch. He's looking at me and I realize Luke had snatched the towel from me and I'm naked.

Max doesn't give me the same look as Luke did or my brother's do. He looks sad and I want to go to him and let us hold each other until all the sadness disappears.

Luke follows my gaze and he begins to thrash and scream.

"Help me! This little bitch is crazy! She's broken

my foot.

I'm going to sue you all and tell everyone what you do with your brothers, Evi!" he screams,

Spoilt brat

I know I have to stop him. Daddy will kill me for this.

I hope Max will forgive me and not tell.

Before I can hit Luke again, Max is taking the boulder from my hands.

No. I need that.

My tummy flutters and I think I may pass out.

He lifts the boulder high above his head and drops it over Luke's.

It sounds like he just dropped a coconut to the ground.

My mouth falls wide open and my chest is beating so fast.

Blood oozes from the wound he's created and wide, dead eyes stare up at us.

"Help me move him, Evi."

That day we formed an unbreakable bond.

I told him about Eleanor while we dragged Luke's body to the grave my brothers had already dug for us.

Eleanor is extra fussy today and I beg Daddy to let me stay home but it earns me a backhanded slap to the face for whining and I'm now on the bus surrounded by kids that don't have the same shadows haunting them as I do.

Daddy didn't even remember my birthday is today.

I only know it's my birthday because Max reminded me yesterday.

He seems excited about it for some reason; maybe it's because I'm a year older and closer to an age when we can run away.

You know when you're different.

I see how other parents are with their children.

Even Max's Mom is affectionate towards him, a contrast to mine. Eleanor is getting so big now; I worry about her.

Her feet cause her pain and Daddy refuses to acknowledge it.

He still insists no one can know about her and I don't understand why.

She's still beautiful. She's still just a baby. She's mine and I love her and don't want her to suffer like she is.

Miss Bloom is a nice teacher and she often gives me an apple in the playground or offers me to talk to her if I ever need to.

What if I told her? Would she help Eleanor? I can't risk Daddy finding out and killing my sweet Eleanor.

The bus slows and the day drags.

I think about Mom not tending to the baby and how badly I need to get home to make sure she's fed and has her diaper changed.

The final bell rings and I rush out of the classroom.

Miss Bloom stops me in the courtyard. "Evi, stay back, please. I have a surprise for you."

No. I don't want to. I can't.

"I can't. My Mom and Dad won't like that."

"Come on, Evi. It will be good for you to catch up. We have a test next week."

"My parents won't allow it."

"I'll call them."

Her face saddens and she pouts.

She's so pretty and youthful compared to my mom, who looks old and worn out by life.

"I'll call them and tell them you need to stay back and study."

No.

"Max is inside waiting."

Max? Why?

"Okay," I tell her and follow her back inside.

She's grinning too hard and it makes me squirm.

She opens her classroom door and Max is inside and he yells,

"Happy Birthday, Evi!" He throws confetti in the air and marches toward me, planting a kiss on my cheek and clipping a badge to my top.

Tears build in my eyes and I'm stunned into silence.

"We have cake," Miss Bloom announces.

No one has ever celebrated my birthday.

I've never had a birthday cake or a badge or confetti.

I lose sense of time, and for the first time in my life, I feel like a normal girl.

When the moon beams through the window, my heart thunders in my chest.

It's so late, and Eleanor will be hungry and waiting for me, and if she's crying, Daddy will get mad, and…

"I need to go home!" I shout, and startle Miss Bloom.

"It's okay, Evi. I told your dad that I'd be dropping you home after study session. He won't have to know. I promise."

It's not him I care about.

Max knows why I need to go and nods his head in agreement.

"It's late. We should get back."

The drive home is full of nervous energy.

I wanted to enjoy a day just for me, and the cake was so good that I went back and had a second helping.

The frosting was pink and sweet.

We pull up at my house and Miss Bloom unbuckles her seatbelt.

"I'll walk you in."

"No!" Max and I bark in unison.

"It's fine.

Thank you for the party." I un-belt myself and climb from the car.

I wait for her to pull away before I go inside.

Daddy isn't in the kitchen or living room so I know he must be down in the basement where he watches those dirty movies that Mom hates.

As I drop my bag in my room and kick off my shoes, I turn to go to Mom's room to see Eleanor.

She's not fussy so maybe she's asleep and Mom fed her today.

Pushing open the bedroom door, I see Mom's form beneath the covers.

There's a strong smell of alcohol and an empty bottle on the floor.

I notice then that Daddy is snoring on the bed next to Mom.

He must have had a bad day.

Please don't wake up. Please don't wake up.

I move to the basinet and it's empty.

Eleanor?

Creeping over to the bed, I search as delicately and gently as possible. She's not there.

"Evi," Lucian hisses from the doorway.

I tiptoe out of the room and he shuts the door behind me.

"Don't wake, Dad. You know how he gets when he's drinking."

No one is safe from his belt when he drinks too much.

"Where's Eleanor?" I ask, my voice cracking.

He squints his eyes at me. "Where have you been? That thing cries all the time. I needed to shut her up."

I'm going to be sick.

"Where is she?"

"It was an accident."

No. No. No.

"Where is she?" I scream, and his eyes spring wide and his hand comes over my mouth to shut me up.

I pull away from him and run to the kitchen.

"She was making too much noise!" Lucian bellows, following me.

Prince comes from their room and shushes us.

"You're being really loud. Dad will wake up."

"Lucian did something to Eleanor!"

Prince's gaze turns to our older brother. "What did

you do?"

His skin blanches and his hands ball into fists. There's a tremble in his lip that gives away that he's scared.

"She was making too much noise. I just wanted her to stop crying."

I'm dying. He's done something bad; I know it.

"Where is she, Lucian?" Prince asks.

"What did you do?"

"I put a pillow over her face to shut her up. I hate looking at her," he growls.

No. No. No.

"She was blue when I went back in to check on her."

"You killed her?"

The room spins around me and I don't think I'm breathing.

"Dad is going to kill you," Prince breathes.

"No he isn't. I took her to that lake that Evi is always playing in. You will tell him it was an accident, that you did it."

I'm out the back door before he's even finished his words. My head is going to explode.

I don't even remember the journey to get here but I'm standing at the lake edge, searching.

It doesn't take long. Her tiny body floats, face down.

A fever takes over me, boiling my blood.

They killed me years ago and then my Eleanor came and gave me something to hold onto.

I don't want to be here anymore.

"Oh my God." Max's hushed words crawl over me.

He's wading into the water towards Eleanor.

I don't want him to get her. Let her be cleansed from this cruel world.

"She's dead. Oh God, Evi."

The limp weight of her body cradled in his arms is torture to see.

"This is my fault," I choke.

A scream rips from me as I fall to the ground.

"I left her with them and ate cake." My insides twist up and break. "They killed her because she was in pain and hungry. I didn't come home to feed her." I can't catch my breath my head is humming.

"Who did this?" Max's eyes water; he's crying too.

"Lucian," I breathe, a weird feeling coming over me.

The tears stop and all I want to do is kill them.

Crush their skulls like Luke's.

"Evi, why does she look like this?" Max asks, looking down at my poor, precious, Eleanor.

"Daddy said she's deformed, that's why we can't tell anyone about her." It doesn't make sense to me.

Other people have children with deformities; they're a little different but all special and nothing to be ashamed of.

It's probably all those drugs mom takes, I looked it up once at school, I think it's something called a cleft palate.

I love Eleanor.

Others would love her too, or would they see her as Lucian did and just want to shut her up?

There's a pain in my chest, so sharp.

"This has to stop."

I hear Max calling to me as I rush back to the house.

I creak the back door open and no one is up; the house

is still.

Lucian and Prince didn't even care enough to wait for me to come back in.

Like Eleanor is not even human to them and that horrible pig didn't kill her.

A darkness clouds my head and I walk in a state of careless abandon.

My hand slips over the handle of the kitchen knife I use to make them all sandwiches.

Max is whisper yelling my name at the doorway of our house.

He's never been allowed inside before but he comes in and grabs my wrist.

"Evi?"

I stare into him, letting him know how broken I am and how I need this all to stop.

His grip drops from my wrist and I make my way to the boy's bedroom. It's not late enough for them to be sleeping.

I push open the door and Prince looks up at me from his bed.

He's lying down, reading a magazine.

Lucian isn't in here and my heart hammers in my chest.

"Did you find her?" he asks, like I was looking for a lost pet that escaped the yard.

His eyes expand and he attempts to sit up when he sees I'm not alone.

I rush him, lifting the blade high and plunging it down into his chest.

He doesn't know what's happening and he's too shocked to scream out or stop me.

The knife sticks in his chest and it's hard to pull out.

He's gurgling and blood coats his bottom lip.

He's choking on my name and it's beautiful.

I tug and pull on the blade but I can't dislodge it.

He tries to slap at my hands but he's too weak.

Max's body heats behind me as he covers his hands over mine and he uses his strength to help me pull the knife free.

I smile over my shoulder at him and stab back down into Prince over and over.

His blood sprays up at my face and then a scream resonates from the doorway.

Lucian stands there in the doorframe, mouth slack.

Max rushes him and crashes into his waist, knocking him to the floor. They spill into the hallway and I run after them.

Max lands a fist to Lucian's jaw but Lucian is much bigger and tosses him off like he's a rag doll.

He doesn't see me coming though, and doesn't have time to prepare when I lunge and pierce his cheek with the knife; it slides in like I'm carving meat for dinner.

His hands try to grab at the blade but he cuts himself on it and I jiggle the blade and pull it free, stabbing into him over and over and over.

The warm blood coats my body and I scream and scream as I plunge and punish him.

For Eleanor, for me.

Movement sounds from my parents' room and Max

grabs me under the arms and lifts me up.

My legs flail and kick.

I don't want to stop.

Lucian deserves it.

"I'm not done." I gasp.

"Evi, let your parents take the blame. Make it look like they did this, otherwise you'll be taken away from me," Max pleads, fear blazing in his eyes.

"He needs to die too," I tell him.

There is no choice; Daddy needs to be punished too.

He closes his eyes and they re-open with a sparkle that tells me we're the same person, same soul, same darkness.

"Give me the knife," he orders, and I hand it over.

Following him to my parents' room, the door swings open under his shove and they're both still in bed.

Max walks to my Daddy's side and I use my finger to draw it across my throat, showing him what I want.

He nods his head and does exactly that.

Blood squirts up the wall and my pulse races.

Daddy's body jerks around and then nothing.

So easy.

Bye, Daddy. Rot in hell.

Mom doesn't even wake up. She's so far gone; always did ignore the blood being spilt in this house.

"And her," I tell him, walking over and standing over Daddy's body. I watch, transfixed, as the blood pumps from the slit across his neck.

"Do her," I tell Max, but he's shaking his head.

He hands me the knife.

"No. She did this. That's what you'll tell everyone."

"No" I argue, clutching the blade. I'll do it myself.

"They will take you away and we will never see each other again," he pleads with me.

"I don't want them to have Eleanor!" I cry.

They will bury her with them if Mom tells people about her, and they don't deserve her.

"We can bury her. No one knows about her. No one has to know," he tells me.

"No one will believe anything your Mother says. She's delusional."

He moves over to the bed where mom sleeps and smears dad's blood on her.

"Bring me the knife, Evi." He holds his hand out.

I move to walk around the bed to him but Daddy's blood has spilled over the side of the bed and my foot slips in it and I drop forward onto the knife in my hands.

The sharp pain burns and stings through me. I gasp.

Max calls out to me.

Spots dance in my eyes.

Max is carrying me; I feel like I'm floating.

We're outside. He stands me up next to him and my stomach hurts so bad I don't think I can stand.

"Stay with me. I'm going to get my mom."

"No." I clutch his arm. "Eleanor. Bury her, Max. Please."

"You're bleeding bad, Evi." He looks over my injury.

"I don't think you can have hit anything important. Mom made me learn all her nurse crap about the human body but I can't risk it. Please let me get her," he mutters, and the cold nips at my skin.

"No, Max. Bury Eleanor for me. Please."

Condensation pushes steam from his lips. "I'll bury Eleanor and call an ambulance."

And then I'm alone and my body needs to lie down.

The floor is so cold, the night dark.

I'm dying.

CHAPTER TWENTY-TWO

ME

"What do you remember about this Eleanor?" Garret asks.

I remember her death was so painful, it was like my soul caught fire and the flames blackened my heart. The ash of my spirit rained down like dirty snow all around me. Ice cold and dark, changing me forever.

His arms move to rest on his knees he leans forward and assesses me; always assessing.

"There was no body recovered for a girl and no record of an Eleanor, Evi."

Of course there wasn't.

She's buried by the lake, at peace.

Max.

"Do you hear voices in your head?"

No. All the voices are dead.

"No."

It is the cruelty of life that keeps a heart beating through heartache. Pumping just enough to warrant your entire being to shrivel up and cry out in the agony of it, and just enough to keep you present, alive to feel it all.

I protected myself from that pain and let my mind erase everything else along with it.

Max.

"So what happened to Eleanor, Evi?" Garret asks, but I'm done talking. I'm done with therapy. I don't need it.

My Eleanor was a beautiful angel born with defects due to our mother's addiction.

Now I know why our father was scared for people to find out about her, he thought his incestuous relationship with his sister caused her birth defects.

I wish I could kill them all, all over again.

Getting to my feet, I outstretch my hand to him.

His brow furrows and he copies my movements.

"Thank you for everything."

"We still have lots to …"

I hold my hand up to stop him.

"No, we're done. I'm okay."

I smirk and leave him watching my retreating form.

I burst out of the door and Max jumps to his feet.

He's been sitting out here, waiting for me.

He's always been waiting.

In the light of his appraisal, I grow tall, wild, and

assured in my vengeance.

My eyes drag over the reflection of myself in the mirror behind him and she grins back at me.

Underneath all the confusion and doubt, I was hiding all along, just waiting to be pulled through the wreckage of my past.

Max uncovered me amongst the murky waters and reminded me who I am.

I'm resilient. I'm vengeful. I'm whole.

I'm Evi Devil.

And I have the wings and the horns to prove it.

EPILOGUE

MAX

This reception room is bland, you'd think they'd make it cheerful but it reminds me of a principal's office, and my feet are itching to get out of here. Not without her

Waiting for Evi to come back into my life was like living with a shadow over my heart, It had been so long I almost believed I dreamt her and the darkness I allowed to seep from my soul was just ink spilled on the lake water she loved so much.

The door bursts open and my girl is standing in the doorframe. There's something different in those mesmerizing dark eyes of hers, clarity maybe? Jumping to my feet every fiber of my being hums to go to her, collect her in the safety of my arms and shelter her from feeling pain, confusion, and sorrow ever again.

I don't want her to remember Eleanor because of the heart-wrenching grief that will follow, but Eleanor also deserves to be remembered, and I visit her gravesite to tell her how much she was loved by her big sister and that the people that betrayed her and neglected her paid the price for their cruelty. No one should ever have to dig a grave that small and her soul will forever remain a part of me because of it.

My gaze re-focuses on Evi, the curl of her lips, she's smiling, and it almost knocks the wind from my chest. She's so beautiful. If she is an apparition, I never want her to fade.

I knew even at such a young age that she was different, a chaotic soul of fragmented pieces that needed someone to hold them in the palm of their hand and show her they wouldn't crash her further, that with those pieces, she created the perfect picture.

And then when she appeared back in my life like a ghost from my dreams, I became instantly drunk on her, captivated by her eyes and addicted to the sound of her heartbeat, when I listened closely enough, I'm sure it whispered my name.

She said she had done something bad back at Greenfields but she doesn't realize we both have done things that other's wouldn't understand, they don't need to. I would ` do anything and everything to give her vengeance, peace, a small piece back of what they stole from her.

Staying in her presence when she came back to me despite her not remembering what we did was a gamble, what we did to free her was a risk but observing at her looking up at me, I've never been surer of anything, I'd do it over and over again for her.

If there were a thousand worlds

And I had a thousand lives

A thousand hearts that beat

I would find her

Love her

Choose her.

With our darkness and light combined we create an endless night sky and together we will soar.

Her arms wrap around my neck, and I have to lean down to place my lips against her neck.

"I remember them. Her. You." She breathes her warm breath misting over my cheek.

My heart constricts at her words waiting for her to tell me it can beat again.

"Thank you." She exhales.

Thud.

The END.

ACKNOWLEDGEMENTS

A huge thank you to you the reader, for picking up this title and reading through until the end.

This book captured my heart and Max and Evi became fast favorites for me.

I hope you enjoyed their dark love as much as I did. It's surprising what we're willing to do for another being when you love them so intensely.

Writing always takes me away from my family at times and they're wonderful and supportive so as always I want to thank them for letting me be me, and take the time to set the voices free.

These books don't happen on their own, so a BIG thank you to Kyra Lennon for coming on this journey with me and working along side my chaotic schedule.

She loved this story and I need the reassurance so thanks for stroking my ego. Haha!

Thank you to my Beta readers who pick up any little things I miss.

Charlie Chisholm, Emma White, Nicky Price, Rosa Saucdo and a special mention to Taylr Hasket, my new beta, glad to have you on board the crazy train.

As always Stacey over at Champagne formats for always making my books beautiful.

Big thank you to Terrie and my girls in my darKER group for keeping me relevant in the smoggy world of social media.

The cover created by Amy Queau is perfection as always.

Thank you to all the incredible blogs who share the love for my titles, without you, I would struggle to get titles out there in the hands of eager readers.

Thank you to everyone who makes time to leave a review, I can't express enough how important reviews are so thank you.

Big shout out to my wonderful group members Dukey's darKER souls, thank you for all your love and support.

Special mention to, Nicky and our new admin Rosa who keeps the ship running.

And Terrie my PA who keeps me running. I love you.

A special thank you to Kirsty Moseley who always has time for me when I need a chat and reads my work for me when I need an opinion on things.

I feel so lucky to have you in my inbox ← Sounds dirty right?

Thanks for being my friend.

ABOUT KER DUKEY

My books all tend to be darker romance, edge of your seat, angst filled reads. My advice to my readers when starting one of my titles…prepare for the unexpected.

I have always had a passion for storytelling, whether it is through lyrics or bedtime stories with my sisters growing up.

My mum would always have a book in her hand when I was young and passed on her love for reading, inspiring me to venture into writing my own. I tend to have a darker edge to my writing. Not all love stories are made from light; some are created in darkness but are just as powerful and worth telling.

When I'm not lost in the world of characters I love spending time with my family. I'm a mum and that comes first in my life but when I do get down time I love attending music concerts or reading events with my younger sister.

News Letter sign up: http://eepurl.com/OpJxT
Website: www. authorkerdukey.com
Facebook: www.facebook.com/KerDukeyauthor

Contact me here
Ker: Kerryduke34@gmail.com
Ker's PA : terriesin@gmail.com

KER'S BOOKS

Titles by Ker include:

EMPATHY SERIES
Empathy
Desolate
Vacant
Deadly

THE DECEPTION SERIES
FaCade
Cadence
Beneath Innocence—Novella

THE BROKEN SERIES
The Broken
The Broken Parts Of Us
The Broken Tethers That Bind Us—Novella
The Broken Forever—Novella

THE MEN BY NUMBERS SERIES
Ten
Six

DRAWN TO YOU SERIES
Drawn to you
Lines Drawn

STANDALONE NOVELS:

My soul Keeper
Lost
I see you
The Beats In Rift

THE PRETTY LITTLE DOLLS SERIES:
Pretty Stolen Dolls
Pretty Lost Dolls
Pretty New Doll

TITLES COMING SOON:
Lost Boy
Pretty Broken Dolls

28840777R00149

Printed in Great Britain
by Amazon